THE FAMILY AT DITLABENG

By the same author

THE
FAMILY
AT
DITLABENG

Naomi Mitchison

Illustrated by Joanna Stubbs

An Ariel Book
FARRAR, STRAUS & GIROUX   NEW YORK

jM6967fa

Author's Note

The Bamatsieng, whose tribal capital is Ditlabeng and whose chief is Letlotse, are a tribe that some of us in Botswana invented. I wrote about them in an adult book called *When We Become Men*. But the other tribes I speak about are real. The Bakgatla, of whom I am one and about whom I wrote in *Friends and Enemies,* have their tribal capital at Mochudi (page 92). Our neighbors on the west are the Bakwena. Our other neighbors, the Bamangwato, have their capital at Serowe, where there is an agricultural show (page 69) every year, in which not only animals but pottery, carving, leatherwork, and so on, from all over Botswana, are shown and may get a prize.

A ward (page 40) in a Motswana town is the part where originally one big family group settled. But these grew and grew and now it is difficult to tell where one ward ends and another begins. But the headmen who settle ward disagreements and allocations of land for housing and so on know quite well.

Botswana is the country. Batswana are the people of the country; Motswana is the singular from this plural. Setswana is the language.

Contents

Contents

THE FAMILY AT DITLABENG

1

No Money

There are hundreds of children in Ditlabeng. They play all over the town, but in the hot weather they do most of their playing on the nights of the full moon. It is light enough then to catch the other runner, or to see what is going on in a game of pretend. It is light enough for skipping or stick games, or ball games if you have a ball; above all, light enough to see a snake if there happens to be one slithering across, to see it and kill it if one can, or else to shout for an older brother. But however bright the moonlight is in the open, it is still dark and secret under the great

3

shade trees, the *morulas,* which in their season drop golden-green fruits all over the ground, ready to be picked up and eaten.

Most of the children don't start school until they are eight or nine, and some don't start school at all. School is not free in Botswana, as it is in Europe or America. Botswana is a poor country. So going to school costs money, and sometimes the money isn't there, not even the few shillings a term which is what going to the primary school costs. People can always have land to plow and raise a crop; that is their right as members of the tribe, and they pay no rent. But when there is no rain, the corn withers in the ground. When there is no rain, there is no grass and the cattle die.

A man may be rich one year, with a hundred cows and oxen, perhaps more, and sheep and goats as well. When he kills an ox, many of his friends come and eat with him. His wife goes to the store and buys what she needs. She brews beer often; there is singing and happiness. When they kill their pig, she makes plenty of soap from the pig fat. Then the big girls help her fetch the water; everything is washed. The children of that house go to school—all the children. The boys wear clean shirts and shorts, the girls wear gym tunics and white blouses.

4

No Money

But a bad year comes—or worse, two bad years, perhaps even four bad years. Then a man may be left with no cows and no oxen. There is not even an ox team to plow his land. He has hardly a goat left to give milk. When that year comes, his wife cannot go to the store; there is no money for tea or sugar or lamp oil or matches. There is no money for smoking tobacco for the men or snuff for the old ladies. No money for a blanket or a kettle. No money for medicine at the hospital if someone is ill. No money for school.

The children playing around Ditlabeng know all this because it is part of life, but they do not know it too hard until it hits them. When times are fairly good, they do not have to know. If one of them has a rich father, he may get some sweets from the store. He will run out with them and then all his friends will share till the sweets are finished.

There is room to play everywhere in Ditlabeng because the town is spread out all over the flat ground between the rock ridges of the hills and on ledges halfway up the hills too, just where someone decided he would like to build a house. Most of these houses are round and neatly thatched, standing on a round base with the thatch coming down over it, so that you can always find somewhere to sit on the step, during summer in the shade, but in the sun during the cold winter months. All the houses stand in a *lapa,* a courtyard with a low wall and a smooth clay floor. Sometimes a big family has several houses in one *lapa,* and perhaps a granary like a little house as well. In one corner there is a small hollow for a fire, with pots and a kettle standing by it. This is the nicest place in winter, the place where you can keep warm and hear stories and join in the singing and watch the sparks winding up toward the stars. But the floor of the *lapa* is always swept clean and is always safe for children to play on.

When they are tired of playing, the children come home and there is always something to eat, even if it is only cold porridge. When they get sleepy, they unroll their mats and curl up on them and sleep. How well one sleeps after a day of playing!

But they have to work too. The girls must help Mother, especially with pounding the corn, which is called *mabele;* that is, sorghum. It is the only kind of corn people can grow in such a dry place. The boys must fetch firewood and, as soon as they are old enough, they must herd the goats. But it is fun going out herding with the bigger boys and playing games and learning riddles and at last learning to shoot with the sling you have made yourself.

That was what Kabi did, and his little brother Modise, who was only six, was beginning to go with him. Kabi was

proud of herding his father's goats. He was a big boy, nine years old. They had eight goats. Kabi couldn't count, not yet, but he knew every goat as if it was a person. Herding goats was next best to herding cows. When you did that, you were almost a man. His cousin Sello already went to the cattle post and herded cattle.

But what about school?

Mosaye was going to school. She was his older sister, thirteen years old, a big girl. She was learning arithmetic and geography and English; she brought back little books with pictures from school and read aloud out of them. Sometimes she ordered Kabi about, although he was a boy. She had a blue gym tunic and a white shirt. Her mother washed and pressed the shirt very often and it was beginning to go into holes, but there was no money for a new one. Itseng, the next sister, had started school two years ago, but she had no gym tunic, only an old cotton dress. She knew there was no money for anything else.

The last years had been bad and getting worse: too hot, hardly any rain, although they had all prayed as hard as they could. The crops had been getting poorer and poorer, scarcely enough grain to keep them in *mabele* porridge through the year. The beasts had suffered. Only two calves this year. The oxen were too thin to pull the plow and it was getting late for plowing anyway. In a good year it would not have been too hard to find money for school fees, to pay one's tax, to pay for tea and sugar and paraffin, to buy a new plowshare or a blanket or a kettle or whatever one needed. But not this year. Father had scraped together enough money for the two girls' school for this year. Kabi need not start for another year. Three school fees would be much money, more than he could see coming. And little Modise after that!

Father was worried. Where was this money to come from? Then one day, when there was still no rain, Father, whose name was Letsie, made up his mind to do something that was very hard. He would go for a year to the gold mines in the Republic of South Africa. He had been there once before, as a young man, before he was married. He had not liked it. The work in the mines had been hard and strange; down there in the dark he had been afraid to his bones. But he had brought back money. Yes. Now he had experience and surely they would pay him a little more.

The family were worried too. One or another came to talk it over with him. His brother Mualefe, who worked in the store, came. He had a wage, but not a very big wage; and also he was married and his children too must be fed and go to school.

The two men sat side by side on the step in front of the house, in the shade of the thatch. Letsie had put two real windows into his house. Inside there was a cupboard, a big bed with brass knobs, boxes, a curtain on a string, and, on the shelves, jars and tins which had once been full. Letsie and Mualefe wore shirts and trousers, clean but rather

9

worn; both went barefoot, though Mualefe wore shoes
in the store where he worked because he had been told to.
When you went to the mines, you had to wear boots and
walk on hard stones. But not here in Ditlabeng. Even the

roads of Ditlabeng are soft dust. They are kinder to the feet than the ground between the houses because you don't get thorns growing on the roads.

"You could go next week when they have this train," said Mualefe. "They say it goes all the way."

"That is the same way I went before," said Letsie unhappily, running his hand through the close blackness of his hair, "and it takes long, long, and when the train stops you are stared at as though you were cattle going to market."

Mother listened, sitting a little away from the men. The girls came back from school, slipped into the house, took off and folded up their school clothes, and put on instead their ordinary little string kilts that came halfway to their knees and left their neat little behinds bare. Mosaye wanted to listen, but her mother motioned her away. There was corn to pound for tomorrow. Only she knew that her father had to make up his mind about something very hard and it was because of money. "Stared at like cattle!" he said again.

"And yet Botswana is a country now," said Mualefe. "A free country. Independent, they said."

"All the same, we have to do this. We have to sell ourselves to the mines."

"It is said that Chief Letlotse was speaking to some big

man from overseas. We might have our own mines in Botswana. Someone heard it on the radio."

"It would be good to have a radio," said Letsie, "and very good to have mines. Our own mines in Botswana. But it is not yet. And the children are hungry today."

"If you go I will not let your children starve, my brother," said Mualefe. His wife, Maswe, had come into the *lapa*. She was a fattish, smiling woman; the girls liked her. And now someone else had joined them, coming out of her house at the far end of the *lapa*. She was the other mouth that had to be fed, the children's grandmother, Father's and Mualefe's mother. Many people said she was the best potter in Ditlabeng, but few women wanted her pots nowadays, only just sometimes, when a big beer pot was needed. Otherwise, women would rather buy metal pots and kettles or light plastic buckets. The old pots were heavy to carry on the head all the way back from the borehole. They did not wear out as the plastic buckets did, but still, if you dropped them they broke. So it was not often that people gave Granny shillings for her pots.

She looked anxiously at the two men sitting there, trying to see a way out of being so poor. "My sons," she said, half aloud, "my big sons. They will take care of us." And then she looked toward the girls, Mosaye and Itseng, pounding away at the corn in the tall corn mortar, the beaters rising and falling evenly. Yes, they were good girls.

Not only did they pound corn for the family. Often Mosaye and Itseng helped her, bringing different kinds of clay and mixing them the way she said. But Itseng was no good at making things out of clay. She was careless; she was in a hurry to do other things or go off and play. Mosaye, though, would sometimes manage a little pot by herself, which was well smoothed in and out, and a satisfying shape to hold in one's hand. "You too will be a potter one day," said old Mmaletsie, touching the clay with gentle fingers. But Mosaye made a little face. Who wanted to be a potter and sit all her life outside a house looking at one thing only, a thing which people no longer wanted?

There were times when Mosaye wanted to be a nurse. Or else she wanted to be a teacher. The weekend when the two top classes of the school went in a lorry a hundred miles to Gaberones, the capital of Botswana, she wanted to be a clerk in a government office, or perhaps to sell pretty things in a smart shop. Itseng was not old enough to know what she really wanted. If Mosaye wanted something, so did Itseng.

Certainly they did not want their father to go to the mines. But they also knew that it was the only way there could be money. Mosaye, at least, did not want to drop out of school. But when he went they knew that his brother, their Uncle Mualefe, would be the one they would look to. His middle son, Sello, was their friend. He was the same age as a brother they had once had, older than Kabi, younger than Itseng. But the brother had been bitten by a snake. He was on his way to the cattle post with food for Father. He had not been watching all the time; the snake had struck. When they found him, he was dead.

These things happened. But Sello had taken his place. Kabi looked to him as an older brother. And Mosaye and Itseng often went to help their Aunt Maswe, Mualefe's wife. They would pound corn for her or help her to scrub the wooden bowls with sand. Mualefe had a long-shaped house with three rooms in front and a porch where there were boxes and pots and skin rugs. The house had a tin roof, which was good for water because the rain ran off it into a water tank when there was rain. But if one was in the house during a storm, the noise was terrible and one wished it was thatch.

The oldest of Mualefe's children, Segwai, was a big girl at the secondary school. She was very clever and she wore glasses so that she looked altogether like a teacher. She could do long and difficult arithmetic sums. Often she explained to her cousins things which they had not been able to understand in their lessons. All of them were altogether like brothers and sisters.

2

Clay Cows

How hot it was, how hot! The river dried out into pools, then they too dried into cracked mud. The cattle and goats roamed about looking for water. Mostly it came from boreholes that went far down into the ground; some of these boreholes were owned by groups of families, else people would have to pay for every pailful they took. There were little engines that pumped the water up, but it came slowly. The women and girls had to line up in long rows with their pails, waiting for their turn at the borehole and the precious cool water. Mosaye went once for her mother

17

and then again for her grandmother. She went before school in the morning and often she was too tired to attend to her lessons. Itseng only went once for water, but it was she who started pounding the day's supply of *mabele,* the grain that must be steeped in water and then broken up to make porridge. Mosaye joined in and they pounded enough for Granny too. Most of the girls started the day like that before they changed into their school clothes. Even Segwai, who was in Form II of the secondary school, went for water. Sometimes there was a little porridge left over from the day before, for breakfast, or a drink of goat's milk, but often there was nothing.

There wasn't much else besides porridge to eat, and what was worse, there wouldn't be even after harvest time. In a good year with plenty of rain you would get a crop of *mabele* and also maize so that everyone got plenty of delicious corncobs boiled or roasted. There would be two or three kinds of beans and, for the children, watermelons and sweet reed to peel and chew up and spit out. But not this year. Letsie and his brother, their uncle, had managed to plow half their lands, but after that, it didn't seem worthwhile. When the corn came up, it withered in the sun. There was no rain to make it green and strong again.

Father had a battered old cardboard case. He put in his spare shirt and his Sunday trousers and tied it up with string. He took his blanket. At the mines they gave you a shelf to sleep on, but it was hard if there was no blanket. If things went well, he would have much to put into his case when he came back. To comfort his wife, who was crying, he told her what he would bring back for her: a dress with flowers, a head scarf, an umbrella, and a little bottle of scent.

"And for me?" said Itseng in a half whisper.

"For you," said her father, "white canvas shoes for Sunday. And for your sister, what?"

Mosaye crept close to him and he pushed her gently about. "Perhaps a skirt. A striped skirt with a pocket, to go dancing in, and a striped bag with a gold clasp!"

"I will have a watch!" said Kabi. He and little Modise were standing there beside the girls, wearing nothing but leather belts and flaps. If Kabi went to school, he would have to wear a shirt and shorts, but not yet. "A watch!" he said again. "I need a watch. Yes, and an electric torch and a box of pins. And a knife, and football boots. A knife with two blades, and a corkscrew. And many, many sweets!" Then he saw that his father was laughing at him.

"But you will remember, my husband," said Mother, "the thing that is needed is money for his school. If it is possible."

"I shall see," said Father, and he scowled away from them into the corner of the house. This was too serious for a promise. They had said they would give him money.

20

Wages. It had been all right last time. Yes—but could white men be trusted?

He went away with the others who were going to the mines. Mother stood there and waved and the smile went slowly off her face. In the sling on her back, baby was asleep. Heavy. She went back alone and the sun was hot on her and the dust burned her bare feet. Baby stirred and cried. She reached her hand back and patted him. But her heart was far away.

Granny Mmaletsie came over from her own house. She sat on the step and sniveled. Her son had gone to the mines. Her son. Her son. Itseng stood on one foot and looked at her. Kabi and little fat Modise stood behind her. "My son has gone to the mines!" said Mmaletsie. "And my *Ngwetsi* * cannot give me a cup of tea! My worthless *Ngwetsi!*" Inside the house Mother heard, but there was no tea, no sugar. Granny knew that.

Mosaye brought her a cup of water. It was better than nothing. Then Kabi looked out from behind his sister. "Granny—*Ngoko*—can I have a piece of clay? There is an old dry piece you have not used. It is all dried up, you will not want it—"

"To make oxen!" said Mmaletsie. "What man thinks of anything but oxen? Even a small man." She looked at Kabi hard and suddenly grinned. "You are like your father," she said. "Very well, make your cows, but let your little brother have a small herd."

Kabi grinned back and trotted over to the other house.

* Daughter-in-law.

22

The piece of clay was hard. "You cannot take the water!" said Mosaye sharply. "You did not carry it!"

"He can take as much of mine as will go into that small bowl," said Mmaletsie. "If he brings me sticks. Enough sticks for my fire."

"I will bring sticks!" said Kabi. "Big sticks from up the hill. Yes, many sticks!" and he ran across with the bowl.

Mosaye said, "Miss Mary is back at Ditlabeng. She went to a course, overseas. She has so many maps of the places where she went, maps and pictures. Sometimes she comes to our school; she is not just a teacher any longer, she is an adviser. She does not want us to do sewing all the hours of handwork."

"What then does she want?" said Mmaletsie.

"She speaks about pottery," said Mosaye, looking away.

"Her!" said Mmaletsie with her nose in the air. "Her grandfather had nothing but a flock of mangy goats and now she calls herself Miss Mary! Her father became a clerk, and still he had nothing but goats. Miss Mary! She has never in her life made even a small clay cow!"

"I think she has," said Mosaye. "She went to do this course overseas. In some country. Yes, in Israel. She learned pottery and weaving."

"Weaving? What is that?" said Mmaletsie sharply.

"It is this thing—of making cloth—"

"Not sewing?"

"No, it is taking threads and making them go in and out. She says that very many people—before they had shops and before they were shown to be Christians and bought dresses and trousers in the stores—made cloth by this weaving."

"But not shop cloth. Not shaped to be worn."

"No. Miss Mary says the woven cloth is better. It lasts very long, she says, and it has more beautiful colors. She says people did this before the shops."

"Before the shops, people wore beads and cloaks made of skins. That is so. I tell you."

"But Miss Mary says—"

"Oh, Miss Mary, Miss Mary! What kind of pots does she think she makes?"

"She showed me a pretty one she had made in this place Israel. It had colors."

"Colors? That is not a pot."

"But, Ngoko, it is a pot. Only it is shining like plastic. You will see. Miss Mary asked me to bring her to you. After she had seen the little pot with the lip which I made with you, she asked me this. She knows that you are the best potter in Ditlabeng but she does not understand about

24

the clay here. She does not know how to make your kind of pots. She will sit at your feet."

"Hm." Mmaletsie chewed this over in her mind. "Well, you may bring her. She shall sit at my feet. Pots. Yes, I will teach her to make pots!"

Kabi and Modise had each made a small herd of clay cows. These cows had thick bodies and very short legs but long and pointed horns. A cow should always have beautiful horns—that is what matters. They put the cows into the sun to dry. Tomorrow they would herd the goats like other boys, their father's and uncle's goats. But in the evening, when the goats were driven in, Kabi and Modise would find that their clay cows were hard. Then they would take them a little way off into the fields—into what would have been the fields of Ditlabeng if only there had been rain. Now there was nothing growing in the fields except the prickles and poisonous weeds that not even the goats would eat. But there in the evening, under the grayish-looking trees among the dry bushes which had no berries this year, the two boys would draw out a cattle kraal in the dust and make a little fence all round with sticks. There would be other boys with clay cows. They would make the cows walk and fight with one another. The cows would fight with their long horns. They would play at cows as the evening cooled down and grew dark, play till they could not see their cows any longer. But then the moon would rise, the clear lovely moon, and there would just be light enough to go on playing cows until they were sleepy. The cows too must go back into their dust kraals and a stick put across to keep them safe all night.

3

Fire

When Father was with them, he sometimes went off with his rifle and managed to shoot a buck or even a kudu. He was a good hunter; he knew the signs. He could move as quietly as a lizard or run, dodging out of sight behind bushes. Sometimes the chief asked him to come on a hunt and that was the best of all, for there was glory in it as well as meat. When he brought back game, there would be meat for everyone, for all their friends and relations and neighbors. Father would cut some into strips and rub these strips with pepper and salt and hang them on a tree in a windy place so that they would dry into biltong. This was good eating; they could nibble a little and feel strong. Once too Father had brought back some wild honey from a tree, half a bucket of it. He had brought back some bee stings too, but those he had laughed at. The honey was very good. Itseng and Kabi talked about it still. The uncle who worked in the store was not a hunter, so there were no treats, although everyone was given the same food. When he had meat, so had they. Mmaletsie above all liked meat which had been boiled and boiled in the pot until it was altogether soft, with the fat melted through the lean. That made the porridge go down. But if the pot is to boil for a long time, there must be wood to burn.

It was like this one Sunday. Kabi had been to get wood. Always he came back with stories of his adventures. He had nearly seen a leopard. He had heard a hyena. A stranger had asked him the way. He had seen the track of a big snake in the sand, like a hand pushing now this way, now that. Mother never liked to hear of snakes because she remembered the brother who had been bitten by the snake and died.

There were many lizards in the rocks, different kinds, some with bright colors. If you climbed among the rocks looking for big branches to bring home, you might find yourself staring straight at a great big gray kind of lizard as long as your arm. It would stare back, its throat throbbing, and then suddenly dart away. There were also rock rabbits with serious faces which sat out on the rocks in the early morning or evening but hid themselves in deep cracks and burrows during the heat of the day. Kabi knew them well and knew the birds and the insects, the broken twigs and the tracks in the dust, tracks of beasts and birds and the bare feet of people. But it was difficult to get firewood near Ditlabeng. There were plenty of trees and bushes, but they had armed themselves well with thorns. So he had to go farther out and this took time when he might have been playing or listening to the talk of older people or just staring at whatever was going on in Ditlabeng.

So this time Kabi came back with as much wood as he could carry. Mother looked at it and said, "Get more." He knew it was because Granny wanted to have her meat boiled and boiled, and why must he go back up the hot stony hill? "There is a snake in the rocks," he said. "So big! It is a python."

"It is what color?" said Mother.

"It is red!" he said eagerly.

But Mother looked at him. "Pythons are not red," she said, and then, "I do not think there was any snake. Go

29

and get the sticks." So he went back and Modise trailed along behind him.

The girls were pounding the grain for the porridge. There was one mortar, and the two wooden beaters went together: when one was up, the other was down. Mosaye and Itseng sang a little to keep time. It had been a long way to the borehole for the water, though there was always something to talk about there with the others who were waiting. But every week the water came more slowly; the heat was driving it down and down into the bottom of the borehole. The sound of the pump in the heat was like a pain in the head.

As they pounded, the smell of the cooking meat began to come at them nicely. Oh, meat! What one wanted in one's mouth was the taste and juice of it! "How long, Mother?" Itseng called.

Mother poked it with a stick. "The meat will be long yet. The porridge is ready. You can eat that when you have finished pounding." But who wants to eat porridge when there is meat? Well, perhaps a little porridge while they are waiting and after they have finished pounding for tomorrow.

Now Granny came over from her house, also having smelled the meat. She would have the first taste of it. She too poked in the pot while Mother stood by. She licked the point of the stick. Then she stuck it in again and licked it again. "That was a fat goat," she said. "My son Mualefe did well to kill it. You have no word from my other son?"

Mother shook her head. She knew that the first weeks at the mines were always difficult. No time to get pen and ink to write a letter, or to buy stamps. "All will be well," said Mmaletsie. "When he writes, he will send money. You must buy tea and sugar. I need tea."

So do I, thought Mother, but she said nothing. The old lady must be cared for. There was also Uncle Mualefe's wife's father and mother; Maswe said that the old man had a sore back and could not work at all. Her own father was the headman of a small village. When he came in to Ditlabeng, he too must have tea. And there was no tea in the tin. No sugar. She went into the house. At least she had salt still, and a block of pig-fat soap and needles and thread and some maize meal in a box so that there could be a change of porridge. There was even perhaps a little treacle at the bottom of the tin which might be melted out with water. In a good year her shelves would have plenty on them: tea and coffee, tins of meat and all the rest that one saw in the pictures on the tins. Bags of beans from their own fields, watermelons, sweet cane, everything!

When would there be a good year again? Baby began to cry. She picked him up and cuddled and rocked him.

Kabi had come back. He had sticks. Modise had a bundle of smaller sticks. Would the meat never be ready? Mosaye poured the porridge out into the wooden bowls; soon it would be cool enough to eat. The pot with the meat was bubbling slowly. Kabi poked some sticks in under it; they began to smolder. He got down on to his knees and elbows and blew; now they were flaming a little. "The fire is my friend," said Kabi. Then came a gust of wind and the sticks flared. "The wind is helping me," he said. "The wind is my friend too!" He put more sticks under the pot; it began to boil harder.

"Be careful!" said Mosaye. "Do not make the fire too big!"

But Kabi paid no attention. He wanted the pot to boil harder. He put in a branch of little twigs which caught at once. He jumped up, pleased. Soon the meat would be cooked! But the wind came again, a strong gust of wind, and snatched up a burning branch—oh, where was it going? Kabi yelled, the two girls looked up. They saw the branch whirl up into the air and then come down right on top of the house, on to the dry thatch over the door.

"Mother!" screamed Mosaye, and dropped the beater

and ran for the pail of water. It was at the far side of the *lapa* in the shade of the wall. She had never run so fast! But the thatch had caught. It blazed up in flames and smoke, and Mother was inside with the baby. Hurry, hurry, thought Mosaye, as she lugged the pail across, half running, and balanced it and threw it up, up over the thatch. The water splayed over the fire. Was it out?

Not quite, but now Kabi had run up with a long stick. Mosaye snatched it away from him and poked off the smoldering edges of the thatch, which fell in a heap in front of the door, and there behind it was Mother clutching on to baby with a terrible look on her face. The heap of thatch began to flare—the wicked wind had come back and puffed at it—but Itseng had brought the other pail; they poured it on and raked the heap to bits. Mother got past and caught hold of the long stick. She poked off some more of the thatch and threw up the last drops from the pail of water. Then she began to cry and to call "Letsie, Letsie," as though Father could hear her.

But there were plenty of others who could. The neighbors came running up. Granny was there first of course, and shaking her fist at Kabi. "It was you!" she said. Kabi began to cry, and so did Modise, who always seemed to want to do what his big brother did. Kabi cried worse

33

when his Uncle Mualefe came over. He was running fast because someone had dashed into the store where he worked and told him his brother's house was on fire.

"It was the wind," said Kabi. "It was the wind's fault!"

His uncle stood in front of him. "Kabi," he said, "the wind would not have burned the thatch if you had not been there playing games with the fire. Now listen. Fire is a friend who is two-faced; he can turn quickly into an enemy. You must learn that. I will teach you myself. Come with me." And he took Kabi by one ear and walked away. He stopped by a bush and chose a stick; he broke it off and swished it. Kabi knew quite well that this would be to teach him to be careful with fires. Yes, he knew quite well. So did Modise know. He followed because somehow he knew that the lesson was for both of them.

The neighbors all came and looked at the place where the thatch had burned. "Oh, terrible!" said one of them. "You could have been burned, you could have lost everything!"

But another neighbor, a big woman called Seloi, said, "It is not a very big hole and we will help you. I have two bundles of thatch left over from my own house and you can have them."

"I have a bundle," said another neighbor. "Do not

cry. Our men will put them on and you will have a whole house again."

"When Letsie comes back, you will tell him what happened. You will tell him that his daughters saved his house," said Seloi. Then she went back to her own *lapa* and when she came again she was carrying a big pail of water. She said to Mosaye, "You have saved your house but you have lost your water. If your house had gone on fire, the fire might have spread to our houses. Here—we will give you this water."

How glad Mosaye was! Not to have to fetch water again. "Seloi, you are a good neighbor!" said Mother.

But Granny had poked the meat again. It was soft, it was cooked! There would be meat for everyone. Each of them took a plate of porridge. Mother dug out the meat with her long wooden spoon and gave some to each of them. How good it was! Even baby had a little.

Kabi and Modise came back. They had both been crying, but when they smelled the meat, they stopped. "Have you learned your lesson?" said Mother.

"Yes, oh yes," said Kabi. "I must be careful with the fire. Very careful. I must never play with fire."

"And you?" Mother asked Modise.

"Oh, yes," said Modise. "Me too." And he rubbed his behind and made a face. But his uncle had only given him a very small beating, just so that he should learn. He did not even have to cry, he only cried because of his brother. Kabi had been really beaten. He would not feel like sitting down for the rest of the day, and after this he would be very, very careful about fire. The beating had hurt, but not as much as seeing the thatch on fire and his mother inside the house. "Mother," he said, and suddenly ran over and held on to her.

"You are a worthless wretch," said his grandmother. "But she has kept you some meat."

4

The Cattle Post

Their Uncle Mualefe had two boys at primary school, as well as the big girl, Segwai, at the secondary school. But he could not manage any more. Perhaps when Segwai became a teacher she would be able to help the younger ones. Meanwhile, Sello was not going to school. Not that Sello minded—not yet anyway. He was going out to the cattle post to help like a man. No more herding goats! "Can I go too?" asked Kabi. "I want to go! I want to be a man!"

"Who will fetch sticks?" said Sello.

The Family at Ditlabeng

"Modise will fetch sticks. He comes with me often. The girls will help him. Oh, I must go!"

It was still hot in Ditlabeng. Most of the playing went on in the evenings. You could hear the skipping games, with the girls making up new rhymes to old tunes and those who were listening doubled up with laughter. Itseng was the bride in a wedding game that all her friends were playing. They had talked it over, arguing like grown men and women over who was to be what. The bridegroom was a big boy whose mother worked at the Mission; often she brought back lumps of sugar or pieces of cake or tomatoes that were only a little bruised. He went to school but he was not as clever as Itseng. He lived in the ward of Ditlabeng where the Mission was, so his uncles were chosen to go to her ward and bargain with her uncles. There was plenty of arguing about who the uncles were to be. Itseng said she must have Sello for one of her uncles or she would not play. And it must be done before he went off to the cattle post! The bridegroom's play uncles came over from their part of their village to hers and conferred with her play uncles after duly going through the correct forms of greeting. Then there was hard bargaining over how many cattle his family would give hers, praise and disparagement of the bride—all good practice for the real thing!

At last it was all agreed. On a full-moon night the

marriage would be played out. Because of the bridegroom's
mother, it would be a church marriage, though everything
else would happen as well. One of the older girls had
found a long white petticoat and a butter-muslin veil for
the bride, but best of all the groom had a top hat, and

better than best he had a bag full of cake, pudding pieces, raisins, sugar, and such good things, so that after they had walked singing hymns and other kinds of songs from one place to another, into people's *lapas* and out of them again, with everybody commenting and saying how well they were doing, they could all sit down in the moonlight and hold a wedding feast.

These make-up games were the best kind of all. They taught one how to be grown up. If anything had been done wrong, the grownups looking on would have told them. In these games the children had singing and dancing and everything that makes life nice. Her real wedding, when it came for Itseng, would be no better. But Mosaye looked down on it. She had to learn things—the questions they might ask in the exams—because if you failed, perhaps they wouldn't let you stay on at school. So you had to learn about things which they said educated people had to know. Some of them were things that happened long ago. Not here. Overseas somewhere. And stupid questions about how much twenty apples cost. As though one had money for apples!

A letter came at last from Letsie. He was in a different mine from the one where he had been, but the work was almost the same. In the barracks there were fights sometimes, but he had not fought. He had hurt his foot, but the mine doctor was good. And here was a little money.

It was on a paper that Mother must take to a post office. It came to one rand and fifty cents. What should she do? First she must pay off her small debt at the shop and buy more paraffin for the lamp. The girls complained when there was no light to do their homework for school, and as winter was beginning to come toward them, the days grew shorter. And then? Tea, sugar, a small paper of snuff tobacco for the old lady. Perhaps beans. Oh, they were dear now! When everyone had them from their fields, then they were cheap. Why? Or perhaps meat. If she could find a good piece without bones. How they all wanted meat! Meat was not dear if you could get a piece with only a small bone. She wandered along the counter of the shop; so many things on the shelves, but not for her. She fingered a jersey. If only she could give each of the girls a jersey to wear at school during winter! No, she must not think of that. Each of them had a piece of blanket to wear on the way. The winter wind could be bitter cold, driving the dust till it bit. She too had a blanket for the winter; baby must be kept warm.

There was talk of a cooperative shop at Ditlabeng. In these shops the profits went to you, not to the man who had the store. But these shops did not give credit. It was not for her—not until a good year came, and surely that must happen some day. How much money left? So little, so little. And she must buy a stamp to write to her husband. Mosaye too would write. She begged an envelope from the shop; it had been on the floor but was not really dirty. One of the girls could bring back a piece of lined paper from school.

Sello was away at the cattle post most of the time now. When he came back, he talked about the food there. Some of the grown men were good shots; there was often a buck roasting on the fire, or a big turkey bustard. Above all, there was milk, fresh or sour, not as much milk as in a good year, but still more than they had in Ditlabeng. And one could ride the oxen. There was a big boy, Molotsi, who always rode an ox. When he beat the ox, it plunged about, but he always stuck on. Even when it fought with another ox! One day Sello too would do that.

Somehow Sello always looked well when he came back. His skin was shining. There was fat on his bones. Kabi did not look so well. You could count his ribs easily, and his knees seemed to stick out of his legs. He was beginning to get sore patches on his head. Seloi, the kind neighbor who had helped them with the thatch for the roof, gave Mother the remains of a tin of Vaseline to put on the sore place, but it did no good. Yet if she took him to the hospital, it would cost money. She tried to give him more porridge; he finished it up but it made him no fatter.

Sometimes the girls got food at school. It was a different kind of porridge made from meal that came in great sacks from somewhere else; the sacks had writing on them that said so. It was also said that this meal had good things in it, dry milk and meat. With a ball of this and a drink of water you got through the day well. But sometimes they got it and sometimes there was none. One month a truck would come and leave sacks of meal at the school, but nothing was certain. The only certain thing was hunger.

Sello took Kabi into a corner and spoke to him seriously, almost as one man to another. "Your father has five cows," he said, "but one of them is old. She has not had a calf for two years. Perhaps she will die. There is a young heifer coming on but she is small still. Also she is lively and not easy to herd. There are two calves still sucking their mothers. Look, your father had six oxen but two of them died and another is very thin. That is all you have."

"There are the goats," said Kabi timidly.

"Goats! Modise could herd the goats. I was herding goats when I was six years old. He has been out with you often, I think."

"Did you mean," said Kabi, "that the cattle—that I—"

"Just that," said Sello. "I have been herding them along with my father's, but sometimes I must help the others. I must get wood for a fire or poles for the kraal. Or I must milk, and I am still not so quick. It is time you came to the cattle post, Kabi. Then we could take turns and you could herd my father's cattle as well as your father's."

"Oh, that I want!" said Kabi. "I will speak to my mother."

"And I to my father," said Sello.

Mother did not know what to say. Why was her man not there? Oh, Letsie, Letsie! Cattle were the concern of men. And if Kabi went to the cattle post, would he ever come back and go to school? What should be said, what? And then she looked at Sello, who had eaten meat and drunk milk at the cattle post and who had fat over his bones. Kabi was so thin. Better for Kabi to go so that he also might eat meat and become strong. Life was more than school. Modise said eagerly that he could herd the goats, he could milk the big she-goat, he could fetch wood, he was a big boy! If Kabi went, the more porridge for Modise.

"Very well, Kabi, my son," Mother said. "You shall go to the cattle post."

5

Miss Mary Comes to Tea

The girls missed Kabi. Sometimes Modise did not bring enough wood and then they had to go out and get it themselves. Granny was cross if her fire died down for want of wood, even if she was not cooking. But Mother thought of the milk Kabi would be drinking at the cattle post. It was beginning to be cooler at night; she had given him a blanket to take with him.

One day Mosaye came back from school with Miss Mary. She was very proud because Miss Mary looked so smart; she had a yellow dress with a black belt and a big black handbag, and in the handbag she had some tiny pottery animals, birds and rabbits and a sheep, but all colored and glazed. She had let Mosaye peep at them on the way.

Mother was proud too that Mosaye's teacher had come to her house. She had some of the tea left and she made a cup at once for Miss Mary. When Granny smelled it, she came straight over from her house. Mother made her a cup too, but it was not so strong. They spoke of the weather, how it was that there was no rain, though in the old days there had always been good rains. Well, almost always. They spoke of Chief Letlotse and how it was time he got married instead of running after the girls.

"It is because he went overseas," said Granny. "That makes people be mad."

"But his sister too, she went overseas," said Miss Mary. "And now she is married and also doing great things at the hospital."

"Women have more sense than men," said Granny.

"That is certain," said Miss Mary, and smiled. Then she said: "This child brought me a small pot which she had made. She says she is your pupil, Mma, and it came into my mind that the teacher must indeed make beautiful pots if the child could do so well."

"The worthless child!" said Granny, but could not keep the pride out of her voice.

"If I might see, Mmaletsie?" said Miss Mary.

Granny hesitated. Could Miss Mary be in some way someone from the government who might tell her she was not to make pots? Or who would put a tax on to her? But no, this was only Mary Motsei, whose grandfather had nothing but a few goats! "Very well," she said. "I will show you."

They went over to Granny's house and sat down on the beautiful skin rugs which Mmaletsie had owned for a long time. They had been made by her husband, the father of Letsie and Mualefe, who had been a great hunter and could judge beautifully what skins went well with one another, and whose sewing was most elegant so that his rugs had the same grace as her pots. But he had been dead a long time now. It was many years since he met the leopard. But he had left her two good sons, as well as a daughter, who had married across in Zambia and did not write often.

Miss Mary praised the rugs but she praised the pots still more and asked Mmaletsie whether she would not like to pass on her skill. "That one," said Mmaletsie with a glance at Mosaye, "might make a potter, but she does not care. She would rather work in a shop. Or even for the government!"

"A good potter would have a chance to travel, to go overseas, Mma," said Miss Mary. "That is, if she had also

passed at least her Junior Certificate." She said this thinking that Mosaye would listen and so indeed she did.

"To this same place you went to?" said Mmaletsie sus-
piciously.

"Israel, yes. Or to other countries. I have a friend who
is also a potter; we met on the course in Israel. She was
what they called outside expert. She comes from Denmark."

"Where is that?"

"It is beyond England, Mma. She says there is snow all
winter, cold shining snow. You have perhaps seen pictures.
But people there care very much for pottery and weaving
and glass and making beautiful things out of wood." But
Mmaletsie did not understand. These people in other
countries! "One day perhaps my Danish friend will come
here and look at your pots when I tell her how beautiful
they are."

"Why should someone from overseas want to see my
pots?" said Mmaletsie. "They can buy things in the shops.
They can buy pails and kettles and jugs and basins. They
can buy teapots with spouts on them."

"Many of those things are ugly," said Miss Mary, and
Mmaletsie nodded. Mosaye was surprised; she had thought
only that such things were out of reach and how lucky

were the people who could just go to a shop and point and the thing would at once be taken off the shelf and given to them. Miss Mary went on: "This friend of mine promises she will come to Botswana some day. May she come then and sit at your feet, Mma, as I am doing?"

"Oh, she may come, she may come," said Mmaletsie. "But I do not think she will buy even one of my pots."

"Sometimes," said Miss Mary, quoting a proverb, "it is the stranger going ahead who lights the lamp. And I myself would like to buy a pot. I would like to buy this one with the fluting."

"But that one is a shilling," said Mmaletsie, almost afraid to say it.

"Here is a shilling," said Miss Mary. "And here, Mma, look, are some little animals to guard your house." She took out three of the little pottery animals that she had made herself in Israel.

Mmaletsie picked them up one after another and her face wrinkled into laughter. "They are made of clay like my grandson's cows," she said. "But how do you put colors on to them?"

"It is with glaze," said Miss Mary, but there was no Tswana word for it and Mmaletsie shook her head. "In a kiln. But baked hotter than your pots."

"And then—did you put this glaze on with a stone?"

"No, Mma. If a pot is glazed, one does not have to burnish it. And it holds water; it does not lose the shine although there is water in it for many days."

Mmaletsie shook her head. She had spent so many hours burnishing her pots. Put together, the hours would make days. While she waited for her husband to come back from hunting, she would work with her burnishing stone, the pot between her knees, or while he was sewing a rug, talking a little to himself as he used to do. But Miss Mary had given her a shilling. It was the first pot she had sold for a long, long time and she had many pots piled in her house. Too many. She went inside and came out with a smaller pot that had a pattern all round it on the wide part below the neck, like six arches. "Take this," she said, "granddaughter of the goats!" But she said this with laughing in her mouth, so that Miss Mary did not understand. Anyhow, she was looking only at the pot.

"One day, Mma," she said, "you will show me how you make pots. For this I think is built up in coils?" Mmaletsie nodded. "I have learned on a wheel. It is different. And somehow I shall get a proper kiln made for the schools."

She gave the farewells properly and Granny answered them and so did Mother. Then she went away, with Mosaye

beside her. "Is it true," asked Mosaye, "that if one learns to be a potter, one may go overseas?"

"It is true indeed," said Miss Mary. "And my Danish friend would say the same."

"How would she say it?" asked Mosaye. "What language does she speak?"

"The Danes speak English," said Miss Mary. "That is another reason why you must learn English fast."

"I also thought that," said Mosaye.

I have a shilling, a shilling, thought Mmaletsie. That is ten cents. Ten is many. What shall I do with them? I shall buy a paper of tea, she thought, and then I shall not have to wait until my *Ngwetsi* has guests. I shall boil my kettle and make my own tea. I shall buy a small paper of sugar. But I shall also buy sweets for a ticky.* I shall buy the small sweets of many colors and give them to my granddaughter Mosaye because she has brought a lucky visitor.

* A coin worth two and a half cents.

6

The Lost Cow

Kabi felt proud, herding his father's and uncle's cattle in and out. Sello taught him the right things to say both to the cattle and to the other herd boys, some of whom were grown men, usually relatives of the cattle owners. But in a year when there was little to do on the land because the drought withered all the crops, several of the owners were there. Others came on visits. One of the herd boys, Molotsi, was Kabi's cousin, son of Mother's older brother, who lived in another ward of Ditlabeng. He was the one who rode his ox, even when it was fighting. He had thirty beasts to look after, and soon he got Kabi to help him with them, putting in Kabi's father's little herd with the rest. At first Kabi enjoyed having this big herd, shouting at them, running round, hitting them with a big stick or throwing stones if they scattered. It was harder work, though: the more he did, the more Molotsi ordered him about. There were one or two beasts which were very difficult, especially an old cow with a red-brown head and little white flecks on a reddish coat. If Kabi tried to turn her, she would shake her horns and charge, and he would have to dodge or climb a tree while Molotsi laughed.

And then there was Kabi's own heifer! A beauty too, but she played tricks on him, running off by herself. Sometimes Kabi was very tired in the evening and wished he was back at home, even if there was nothing to eat but porridge. The food was good at the cattle post. The younger herd boys got only the tough bits of meat, but they had good teeth and there were plenty of stones for breaking up bones so that one could suck out the marrow.

One day something bad happened. That big cow which belonged to his other uncle, Molotsi's father, went charging off, her tail sticking up in the air. Kabi ran after her as hard as he could, but she was gone, quite gone. What was he to do? Try and find her, or go back to the herd?

The Lost Cow

He tried and tried; he ran up and down; he climbed a tree, but there was nothing to see but the tops of bushes. He listened carefully, but there was no sound. At last he thought he must go back, but, oh, what should he tell Molotsi, his cousin? When he found the herd again, Molotsi was sitting on the ground carving a stick and singing to himself. The cattle were grazing all around. Should he say anything? Should he pretend he had brought the cow back? He waited and watched. Perhaps she would come back. Perhaps Molotsi would think he had lost her himself. Perhaps he should say nothing? But what if the cow was eaten by a lion?

He decided to pretend that everything was all right. He walked over to Molotsi and admired his carving. Perhaps the cow would come back herself. Surely she would miss the rest. He waited and waited. The shadows began to lengthen. Molotsi told him to gather the herd. And then it was clear that the big cow was missing. When? Where? "I saw her break away—did you bring her back?"

"Yes, yes!" Kabi said.

"How far did she go?"

But he couldn't keep it up—Molotsi was coming at him. He began to cry, he began to run, and then Molotsi had him, shook him, threw him on the ground, hit him

with the carved stick, broke the stick, and got angrier still.

"Get up," said Molotsi in a very frightening way. "Get the cows."

Kabi knew what was coming. He ran around the herd shouting at them; they started to move back toward the cattle post. The setting sun made a muzz of light through the dust between the bushes. He began to drive them. If only Molotsi would say something! If only Molotsi would beat him, even, but do it now—now! They joined with the other herds going back, a big noise of cattle and thicker dust from the hooves. It was almost dark before they were all back at the cattle post and the beasts herded into the kraal, safe from lions and leopards, wild dogs and hyenas. All but one. Then Molotsi took him by the ear, pulled him over to the fire and the rest of the herd boys. He told all of them—all, getting angrier and angrier—and Kabi began crying harder now, the tears running down his nose, down into the sand when they told him to lie down and be punished. If only he was at home! If only the cow would suddenly come back!

At the end of the beating they told him to get up. He was trembling and bleeding a little. It was the worst beating he had ever had. Molotsi threw his blanket at him and then threw a stone to drive him away from the fire and food. He stumbled away from the others and lay on his face.

Sello had not joined in the beating. Nor, for that matter, had any of the younger herd boys. It might be their turn next. After a while Sello backed out of the warmth of the fire with a battered tin cup half full of milk and took it over to Kabi. Poor Kabi gulped it all down, but he was too sore to sleep. Sello told him stories and riddles while the stars moved slowly overhead above the high, dark branches of the kraal wall. Then he said: "We will start early and find your cow. Then all will be well." He had asked two of the other younger herd boys to take their place.

It is frightening to be alone in the Bush in the early morning before it is light. Sello and Kabi were both frightened, but they went on. The wild beasts were still moving and hunting. They heard little feet that rustled and rattled on the dry leaves. They climbed a tree quickly to let three hyenas go by. What they feared most were leopards, but they never saw or heard one. Not that one always did; leopards came before one knew. The stars grew pale overhead and the hot day began to come. They found a few dried-up berries to eat. At last they came to the place where the cow had strayed off. Yes, those might be her hoofprints, a single track going off by itself.

They decided that each of them must go a different way. Both looked hard at the trees and rocks so that they would be sure to know them and come back to the same place. There was a rock like a lion. Sello broke some branches and stuck them in the ground so that they would be still more certain. Then he peeled the bark half off a long twig, twisted it round and set it in the ground, and asked it where the cow was. The bark uncoiled and the end pointed one way. That was fine, but then it untwisted a little more and pointed another way.

"The cow is moving," said Sello.

They went off one at each side of the lion rock. They could not pick up the hoofprints for certain. At first they shouted to one another, then they stopped hearing the shouts. Both were looking at the ground, hoping to see the hoofprints of a single cow by herself, which might be the one they were looking for. But also they would stand still and smell or look at the sky in case there were vultures. It would be terrible if the cow had been killed by a lion or a leopard, but at least they would know. The vultures wheeling and gathering would tell them. They looked around often to see the way they were going, but they could also follow their own feet back, for the paths they were on were not much trodden by other feet and the dust was thick enough to show marks.

It was Sello who smelled and then saw fresh cow droppings. He went on quickly and there was the cow with the red head and white flecks, grazing quietly in a little hollow where there was still good grass. She had found it by herself. Sello was tired and suddenly hungry; he let her graze for a little time while he rested. Then he went around and started to drive her back; she went easily. He had remembered the way so well that it was not difficult. If he was not sure, he ran ahead of the cow to find his own footmarks.

At last he got back to the lion rock and began to shout for Kabi. Where could Kabi have gone? He began to be a little anxious in case Kabi was in trouble—a snake, a leopard—but suddenly Kabi ran up to him.

"Oh!" said Kabi. "I was lost, I was lost!"

"But you were here," said Sello. "And I have the cow. Look, there she is! We have her back and everything will be forgotten. Do not look like that, Kabi. You were not lost. You were here all the time."

"Here?" said Kabi.

"Yes, here," said Sello. "Look, there is the lion rock."

Kabi looked and his face stopped being frightened. "Before you came," said Kabi, "that rock was different. It was a man looking at me. A wicked man. A witch."

"And there," said Sello, "are the branches I put in, so that we would know for certain."

"They were not there before!" said Kabi. "I was altogether lost."

But suddenly Kabi felt happy. His back was hardly sore any longer. They were going with the cow to the cattle post. Perhaps the other herd boys would stop being angry. Perhaps even Molotsi would be pleased!

"Oh, I was lost," he said again.

"You were not lost," said Sello. "You were only stupid. You were stupid because you were frightened. But now you need not be frightened any longer, and I have your cow. Let us go back. They will give us milk and perhaps meat. Come, Kabi, and don't be stupid again."

7

The Donkeys and the Pots

Winter came on them. But Father wrote again and sent a little money. The Mission had a jumble sale and Mother got two jerseys for the girls. One had so much wear that it would do for two winters. She also got a cotton dress for Mosaye, who was getting too old to wear a kilt out of school; it was made of a hard kind of cotton cloth, bunchy and stiff when the belt was on, but it would last a long time. Mosaye was pleased with her striped jersey because it was not nice to be cold at school, and yet she somehow thought, why was it because one was black one could never have beautiful new clothes like the people in the newspapers? She spoke of this once to her grandmother, who said that in the old days men and women wore beautiful skin cloaks, soft, warmer than these wool things which had once belonged to the white women at the Mission, handsome.

"My mother also," she said, "had a golden necklace. When I sat on her knee, I played with it. And golden earrings."

"Gold!" said Mosaye. "But what happened to it, Ngoko?"

"There was a year of great hunger," said Granny and her face suddenly went hard.

"Worse than this year?"

"This year—it is nothing! We are not yet eating the bark of trees or killing the dogs."

"Did people do that—truly?"

"They did, my child. And that year most of the women who had gold lost it. They took it to the store—in those days there was only one store in Ditlabeng—and got perhaps a bag of meal for a necklace or a bracelet. But their children ate and did not die. It was so."

How can I get out of this, thought Mosaye, and spoke to Miss Mary, who always liked to tell about going overseas and the many cars and bicycles and radios and the light everywhere at night and the way that the white people spoke, as though one were their sisters. But this must be earned by hard work. By passing examinations. By practicing spelling and arithmetic. "Yes," said Miss Mary, "and you must also learn from your grandmother. When did you last make something with her?"

Mosaye decided she must practice on clay as well as in exercise books. She must learn to build up a pot so that it would stand really straight. She must crinkle the lips so that all the crinkles were even. It was difficult. To do this and also to do her homework! But one day Miss Sarah, the chief's aunt, came in and bought a flat dish and spoke to Mmaletsie about sending something to the Agricultural Show over at Serowe. Mmaletsie listened but did not promise, but she made the children get her more clay and she began working. Modise had to get in enough wood for firing; it would not do if that had to be cut short.

Itseng's "bridegroom" helped sometimes, and another boy called Tsheko, whose father had six donkeys. These donkeys pulled a sledge sometimes, or a cart that Tsheko's big brothers had made with two old car tires and some boxes. Tsheko's father had a team of oxen too; he loved them but he did not at all love his donkeys. He thought they were ugly and stupid and sometimes he hit or kicked them. But Tsheko himself loved the donkeys and used to try to find them food; the poor donkeys ate almost anything. And the donkeys were fond of Tsheko. When they saw him, they came up and rubbed their noses against him. They had soft, velvety noses and Tsheko had names for all of them which they knew. He had been at school for three years, but then he had failed an exam and his father would not keep him on. He missed school sometimes and then he would ask Mosaye what she was learning now.

The day came when the pots were fired. The next day, after the ashes were cold, Mmaletsie uncovered the pots very carefully. One or two had gone out of shape. Another was cracked. Others had dark marks on them which Mmaletsie did not like, though Mosaye thought they looked handsome and had a secret feeling that Miss Mary would like them. But there were several good ones and of these one was a lipped bowl which Mosaye had made all by herself.

"You will tell Miss Sarah she can come and choose," said Mmaletsie.

There was a great deal of talking. Miss Sarah had a box and much paper and she carefully packed some of the pots and bowls. How much Mosaye wished she could get to the show at Serowe and see the beautiful cows and horses and the things which people had made, and listen to the choirs! There would be a choir from the secondary school where she would go next year—if all went well in the examination and if there were places. If she got a first- or second-class pass, all would be well, but if she only got third class? Perhaps if she prayed—?

Miss Sarah said she would carry the pots carefully all the way to Serowe. Chief Letlotse would drive and there would be as many people as the car would hold, but the box with the pots she would take on her knee, and she would stop the chief from driving too fast over the parts of the road where the bad holes were.

"Perhaps next year," said Mother, "Father will be back with money from the mines and then we shall all go to the Serowe show. Perhaps it will be a good year, with rain. Always he said that we would go one year."

But a few days later there was bad news. Chief Letlotse had had an accident with his car. He had run into a lorry. Or perhaps a cow. Or a tree trunk. He himself was driving. And he had taken too much to drink. The older people shook their heads; he had been with the young ones at the show. They knew nothing, they could only drink beer and brandy and sing songs. So now see what has happened!

Miss Sarah came to Mmaletsie's home limping because

she had been much bruised in the car, and there was a piece of adhesive plaster on her hand.

"Your pots won a prize," she said. "And here is the money. But I was taking them back to you so that people would hear of your prize and come and buy from you. The box was on my knees and the car had this accident. And they are all broken. All. I am sorry, Mmaletsie. Here is the prize money."

The prize was half a rand; Mmaletsie took it quietly but she was sad about the pots. She wished now that she had said to sell them if possible at the show. But she had wanted to see them again, especially if they had won a prize for her. And now they were all broken. She shook her head.

Chief Letlotse came back to Ditlabeng angry and a little ashamed, and his car did not go so well. Perhaps he had twisted the axle a little. But he would not admit that he had made even a small mistake. He was even angry with his uncles and still more with his aunt, Miss Sarah, whom he had hurt. People kept out of his way. A chief should not get angry and speak bad words to people, especially those who are older than he is.

They heard about it at the cattle post. News travels fast, especially bad news. But it did not matter. What mattered was that there should be enough water for the cows. The flecked red cow had had her calf. How terrible it would have been, thought Kabi, if I had lost her altogether!

One day Chief Letlotse was coming back from Craigs, which is the town where some of the meetings are held and which he had to go to sometimes. It was not a beautiful town like Ditlabeng, where the houses are just where people want to build them, with shade trees and brown thatch. Craigs was an ugly town with a tight row of mean little shops and the houses of white people lined up along straight streets. It had offices, and the railway line went past it, and there were bars full of people drinking and quarreling, and a small factory. Chief Letlotse drove back quickly and angrily. Things had not gone the way he had wanted at the meeting and the garage had not done anything to help the noise that was coming out of the inside of his car. This car of his had not been itself since having the accident. Sometimes he wished it was a horse.

He came around the long corner into Ditlabeng. Tsheko was at the corner with his donkey. He was just loading some wood on to the sledge and then he would harness up the donkeys. Itseng and her "bridegroom" were helping him; sometimes the bridegroom teased her that she was his wife but did nothing for him, and sometimes he gave her things from the Mission kitchen. Then they would do things together for a little. They watched the car coming fast and then suddenly a goat ran across the road. The chief swerved to get past it, but the car did not go properly back on to the road; it twisted, went into a bad skid right

off the road over the low bank and into the bushes. Then
it stopped suddenly and the wheels were deep in the sand.
They could not grip. The chief got out and looked at it.
He tried to push it back but it was stuck. He seemed to be
speaking to himself with bad words.

Tsheko wondered what he would do.

"Do not move," said Itseng. "The chief is angry!"

"He will speak angry words to us," said the bridegroom, "even if we are doing what is right."

Well, it could not be helped. Tsheko ran over and half knelt, and asked Chief Letlotse if he should try to pull out the car. "I have a team of donkeys," he said.

"Donkeys!" said the chief. He sounded very angry. Then he looked at Tsheko and he seemed less angry.

"Wait!" he said. "If my car will go, I will not have to be pulled by donkeys."

He got in and tried to start the car but it would not come alive. Itseng and her bridegroom pushed, but it was no use. The car wheels were stuck in hot, deep sand. They all got down on their knees and tried to clear it away. The chief did it with them and it was only nice words that he said to them. But it was no use. The car would not move. The self-starter of the car was dead, but that happened very often. They looked at one another.

"Very well," said the chief. "Fetch your donkeys!"

Tsheko ran over and brought up the donkeys and their harness. He tied the reims * to the bumper bar of the car. The donkeys got into line and Tsheko called to them by

* Leather ropes for harness.

The Donkeys and the Pots

their names to pull, and so they did. They pulled hard. Itseng and the bridegroom pushed behind. And suddenly the chief was laughing. He was back to what he should be.

The car moved slowly in jerks. The donkeys pulled it through the sand and down the bank on to the road. Tsheko unharnessed them. Then the chief reached into the car; he had a paper bag on the seat beside him. It had thick sandwiches and a piece of cake and an orange. He had got these things in Craigs to eat on his way, but he had been too angry with his car to do any eating. He took them out and gave them all to Tsheko.

"But see that the donkeys get some," he said. "And tell them in their big ears that they are clever beasts." And he patted the nose of one of them before he got back into the car.

But the self-starter was still not working. All three of them had to push the car until at last it got going. The chief leaned out of the window and waved to them and smiled. He was their chief again, their father back again to what he should be—kind to his children, with good words. They all looked at one another and nodded, thinking the same thing, before they opened the bag.

The sandwiches had beef and ham in them. They ate

77

all the beef and ham, but Tsheko kept six sandwich lids, one for each of his donkeys. It was a good thing that the bread was cut so thick. They divided up the cake between them and peeled the orange. It was lucky that two of the donkeys liked orange peel.

When Tsheko got home, he told his father what had happened. He told him that the chief had patted the donkeys. Soon everyone in the village would know and they would all come to look at the donkeys.

"Well, well," said his father. And he looked in a surprised way at the donkeys who had helped the chief.

8

Being Poor

Winter ended as quickly as it had come. The heat began to build up. You did not any longer want a blanket at night. People began to think about their lands and going out to plow and sow the crops. But would there be rain? Before he left, Letsie had agreed with his brother that he should plow both their lands. But the plow oxen were still thin and would need some good feeding before they were strong enough to pull the plow; it would not be worth hiring a tractor unless there was good rain. But if the rain did come, it might be hard to find anyone willing to rent them a tractor or even to get on to the government list for one of their tractors. Most likely they would have to use their own oxen. But first, before anything else, there must be rain.

Baby was beginning to walk but Mother went on feeding him with her own milk. If she did not do that, he would most likely die. The one before him had died when she had stopped nursing her and there was so little other milk. She did not want this one to die. The one before had been a girl, younger than Modise. They had put her into a coffin with brass handles and buried her; the coffin had been dear to buy and they had been sad. Mother wanted this one to be living and strong when Letsie came back. But when—when? It was a long time since he had sent a letter. People were killed in the mines and nobody knew for months. Or they were hurt in an accident and came home with no right hand or perhaps hobbling on a wooden leg. Then they were given a little money. But money did not buy a new hand or a new leg. When Letsie stood upright on his two legs, he was most beautiful. His hands were gentle and clever. If he was hurt—she could not bear it. No.

And there was no money, though after the word got around about the prize, one or two people bought pots from Granny. Yet the family was better off than most; they would be hungry but they would not starve. Mualefe would never let that happen, but his wage was not very big, and if he asked the store for a little more they always said there were plenty of others who would like to get his job. Well—Mother would have to make the porridge go around and if there was little to eat with it, that was how things were.

There was no chance at all to save toward next year's school fees. Mother had tried to put pennies into the tin but now they were all gone. She must keep the girls on at school, most of all Mosaye. Perhaps it could happen that one day Mosaye might get a scholarship and go overseas as Miss Mary had said. Such things did happen sometimes. And if Mosaye got through her primary leaving examination well, then she would go to the secondary school, and the fees there were big, big. Mother could not even think of them; they frightened her.

Her neighbor Seloi had a nephew at the mine, a young man. One day Seloi came rushing in to shout to Mother that her nephew was back and he had seen Letsie and could give news of him. Mother slung baby onto her back and ran to Seloi's house. She threw her questions at the nephew. Yes, certainly he had seen Letsie and he was well. Yes, he had been working at the same mine but he was not in the same room.

"Room?"

"We are twenty men to a room," the nephew said, "with shelves to sleep on. In winter there is a stove. But there is nowhere to put any one thing you might have— your spoon, your piece of soap, your spare shirt. It is a kind of prison."

"But you can go out?"

"There is a fence all around, but on Sundays you can go to the township. Yes, Mma. If you want. But there is nothing there. It is more boxes full of people working for the whites. All. All. On Sundays you quarrel and have fights. Some sing hymns. And perhaps you think about home. Yes, Mma, you sit on the ground and remember."

"But you get food? Much food? He said one ate three times in the day."

"For that work you must have food. But if you have not worked you have no ticket. It is like this: no ticket, no food. With the ticket you have porridge three times a day. Mostly mealie pap. And beans. And stew."

"Beans! Stew! You are lucky. Letsie gets that?"

"Yes, Mma. But how you must work! All your force on the pick going into the hard rock. Then shoveling out the heavy stuff, your back and arms aching. Work, work.

Then you stand in a line with your basin and the food is shoveled in. You eat. So do pigs eat."

"And here—we are happy and we work when we want, as hard as we want. But we do not eat." Then suddenly she added: "And the extra money? He said before he left that they would pay more because he was there before and he knows this work."

The nephew laughed. "That is a trap. If you sign again for another contract before half a year, you get more money. He waited too long. He starts again at the bottom. Half a year—that is all they give."

"It is long since he sent money," said Mother, half to herself. Baby on her back was crying; she reached back and patted him.

"Perhaps he will bring more when he comes," said the nephew. Seloi said many cheering things and she made tea for Mother and the nephew. It was the second time the leaves had been used, but there was sugar in it.

Mother told them at the store that her husband was well; he would be bringing money. So they gave her a little credit. But almost everyone at Ditlabeng was wanting credit because there had been no harvest. Even the teachers at the schools were finding it hard. People had not paid their taxes, although Chief Letlotse had told them many times that they must do this. That meant there was

83

not enough money to pay the teachers. And so it went. Chief Letlotse himself had gotten no harvest and he was worrying. All the same, he tried to put heart into the tribe and cheer them up. When times were bad, people quarreled more and he had to settle their quarrels. When he became chief, he had had many plans for Ditlabeng—he wanted it to be the best town in Botswana—but if there was no rain and no harvest, none of his plans could come to anything.

Mosaye was crying. The shirt that she wore under her gym tunic had become so thin that it could no longer be patched. But a new one? No, the store would not give Mother credit for that. Perhaps she could buy a piece of cloth, but how did one shape it and sew it? It was one thing to sew a skin blanket, a thing done by men. It was altogether another to sew this white people's cloth. Mosaye had come back from school that day with her shirt torn completely; one of the big boys had pulled at it. She had been scolded.

"If Miss Mary was always at our school she would help," said Mosaye, "but she comes only once in the week. Most days she is at the secondary. And I cannot go back like this. No, I will not go to school!"

"But we have paid for the school!" said Mother. "You

must go!" She was suddenly frightened. It was as though her daughter was walking into a fire.

"And the gym tunic!"—Mosaye used the English word. "It is too short!"

"What can I do?" said Mother. "I cannot put on a piece. Perhaps when Father comes home he will buy you a new one." She too was crying and the apron that she dried her eyes on was also torn and she could not mend it. Mother could make a beautiful, well-curved wall for the inside of a round house out of earth which had been mixed with cow dung into a smooth plaster, or she could make this same plaster into the floor of a *lapa* with a pattern worked into it. Or she could make other patterns with different colors on the *lapa* walls. She could make the kind of string kilt that the girls wore at home so that they could save their school or church clothes. She could make baskets finely woven to hold grain or meal. She could carry heavy loads on her head and walk for miles. She could pound meal and brew beer. Oh, there were many things she could do and which she could teach her daughters! But she could not make or mend these clothes that people had to wear so as to look like whites.

Granny came over and looked at them crying. She had a thought. She had shillings in a small pot which she

counted out. She went to the store. Then she came back to the house. She carried nothing but she looked pleased. She said: "I have been to the goat's granddaughter." She laughed to herself. "She said she will show Mosaye how to sew a shirt."

"You told her? You told Miss Mary? You told her I could not do it?" said Mother. "Oh, I am shamed!"

"Mosaye must go to her and learn. Worthless one, go now!"

"But how?" said Mosaye. "I will learn, Ngoko, but there is no cloth to make a shirt."

"There is cloth," said Granny. "There is white cotton cloth with very small, blue flowers. It is strong cloth; the boys cannot tear it. There is also a button—a shining, blue button. The goat's granddaughter has needles and white thread. My granddaughter will be the smartest girl in the school. She will not mind if the tunic is a little short. It is easier to run."

"Oh," said Mosaye, "oh—Ngoko!"

"And this cloth comes from the making of pots. When she has finished showing you how to make the shirt, the goat's granddaughter is coming to me to learn how to smooth a coil both outside and in and to feel the thickness evenly under her fingers, and I shall need good clay, the best, from the far side of the river. And some of the dark stone, and it must be powdered."

"Yes," said Mosaye, "yes, yes!"

9

The Floods

Rain. Rain. The clouds built up grandly into towering, perpetually changing castles. The lightning flickered, lighting them up from inside, throbbing golden balloons as the lowering sun illuminated them high, high up. Sometimes there were a few drops that dried on the hard ground or barely showed as they steadily evaporated on hot walls or floors of *lapas*. Not enough yet, not nearly enough.

It was the same all over Botswana, not only in Ditlabeng. Everyone was hoping for rain. Every animal, every plant was needing rain. The bushes were dry; their leaves rattled and fell. Nothing was green. And yet, all through the village and far out beyond, the fresh creamy flowers of the *Mologa* strung themselves along the bare twigs of the bushes, the first promise that spring would come and life would ease a little. But before that, dust and then more dust was everywhere. The cattle roamed farther and farther looking for food; the herd boys had a harder time. Sello and Kabi were thin and hard with running. There was a big prayer meeting in Ditlabeng, but nothing came of it. Some people said that in the chief's father's time there would have been a black ox sacrificed and the rain would have come. But nobody asked Chief Letlotse to do this. One who has been overseas for his education no longer likes to sacrifice oxen.

A sad thing happened. Mualefe killed a goat, not a very fat goat, but it was meat. He made a big fire and his wife, Maswe, put the pieces of goat into the biggest pot. Mother had hoped he would give her a piece, half a leg perhaps. That would have done two days. But no. She was not even sure if she would be welcome when she came to the eating of the goat. She and the girls sat back under the walls of the *lapa,* though Mmaletsie sat in front among the older ones and got a nice, easily chewed bit, while Modise had got in beside Tsheko, the boy with the donkeys. His father had come and was telling again the story of the chief and the donkeys, and everyone laughed. If Letsie had been there, thought Mother, he would have told stories about the mine and they would all be listening and the girls and I would have better to eat than these bits of sinew and gristle. She wiped her eyes with the edge of her apron. Would he think of her? He had taken her old photograph, curled at the edges, inside his spare shirt; she was standing proudly with her first baby, Mosaye, in a dress with frills. A long time ago. Letsie, my man, my hunter, I weep for you.

Then Mualefe's big girl, Segwai, came over and sat by Mosaye. "Do you know this?" she said. "Miss Mary says that she has written to this friend of hers who is coming from overseas to Botswana and she has told her there is a gifted potter in the village."

"Oh, that is Granny!" said Mosaye.

Segwai giggled. "That is not Granny. That is you."

"Me? It cannot be. Granny is always scolding me. The last time I was working with her, I thought I had done well. But no! I had made a water jar with a tall neck and handle. It was like a crane. But she said that was not the way to make water jars. I get tired with her scolding me."

"Granny scolds us all. She scolds me for being stupid although I am in Form II and have read all these difficult books which she cannot read at all. Miss Mary says—well, I will not tell you in case you become too proud! Mosaye—you have nothing but an old bone. Come with me!"

Could Miss Mary really have said that? I have shown her any of my pots which were good, thought Mosaye, but some are no good. Yet if this friend comes—oh, I must learn, I must learn. Perhaps somehow I could get out of this. I could become rich. If I became rich, Mother and Itseng would have new dresses. Kabi could come back from the cattle post and go to school. Father—yes, Father would come back from the mines. And then she shook her head. No, it was a dream.

Hot. Hot. The crackle of thunder, sometimes the far-off smell of rain. It was said that there had been rain near Craigs. More rain up by Serowe. All the other tribes had got rain. The Bakwena had got some rain. There was a little rain around Mochudi for the Bakgatla. Why none for the Bamatsieng of Ditlabeng? All over Botswana, people talked about rain. If they had brothers or sisters or cousins in other countries or overseas, all they wrote about was rain. Or no rain. That was all that mattered.

Then one night Mosaye woke to a roaring noise coming nearer. She shook Itseng awake and they clutched one another. The roaring hit the house, which shook in a gust of wind, and after the wind came the rain.

The hard, thick rain churned up all the smells of the earth, the dust turned into mud, the mud began trickling, the stones rolling down in the trickles knocked the earth away, cracks opened everywhere. The thatch dripped, the water tanks overflowed, the mud plaster walls of the *lapas* tumbled, undermined by water. All the night and all the day the rain went drumming on. The dark skins of the children streamed with water. At first they had run out in it, laughing and holding up their arms, singing to the rain, letting the dust wash out of the creases all over them. Then they began to get too wet. Why didn't the rain stop? Why didn't this dark roof of cloud move away?

The river woke up again. It moved. The rushing brown water began to spread everywhere. On the flat ground the houses were on little islands. The younger children had never seen anything like it. The older men and women talked of other floods. It would go, but would it take the road with it?

The rain stopped; the sun was bright and hot, but who cared how hot it was when there was a river to play with? Half the children of Ditlabeng were down by the river. They could feel the mud cool and nice under their toes.

The flood water swirled excitingly with bubbles and sticks coming down in it. In the middle there were bushes and planks and streaks of white foam. One of the girls screamed: there was a snake in the water! They all ran to the bank to watch the snake being swept along by the water. But it was dead, it was drowned. The boys threw stones and hit it, but they could not make it any more dead than it was.

Tsheko had brought his team of donkeys down to the edge of the river. They had been rolling in the mud. Now he threw water over them and scrubbed them with twigs. They drank and tossed their heads and blew at him. It was as though they knew there would soon be grass. The bridegroom was helping him. Then he went down to the river where Itseng and the other girls were chasing one another along the bank. "Ha, my wife!" said the bridegroom, but Itseng only splashed him with water. He tried to catch her but she ran away and scooped up mud to throw at him if he got near. "Goodbye!" he said. "I'm going over to the other side."

"How? Can you swim?"

"Of course I can swim!" said the bridegroom. But none of them could really swim. There was hardly ever enough water to swim in, and when there was, the teachers always told them not to go into the water because they might catch illnesses there.

"Oh, look, there is a kid!" shrieked out Itseng. "It is being swept down by the water—oh, it will drown!" She waded down trying to reach it, but the water was brown like porridge; you could not see through it. You could not see where the sloping bank of sand ended and the real river began.

"Be careful!" the others shouted at her. "The kid is right in the middle of the river. Nobody can reach it!" Tsheko had a long branch for driving the donkeys. He ran up with it and tried to hook the kid and pull it into land. But he could not reach, nor could she. The kid was struggling and bleating. The water was pulling it down. It was trying to swim, but the river was too strong for it.

By now Itseng was in the water right up to her waist. The kid was swirling round. She had nearly reached it. And then she slipped. She slipped off the sandbank where the flood water was, right into the main river. She screamed and splashed but she could not swim. The river was pulling her away. Everyone was shouting and yelling. "She will drown! She will drown!"

One of the other girls shook the bridegroom. "Swim! You said you could swim—go on!" But of course he could

not swim. He waded out lower down, but when he began to feel the river pulling at him, he was afraid. The river was rolling Itseng over and over; sometimes her head went right under. She would drown! It was terrible, they would not look at it! The younger children ran away screaming, but the tearing floods had hollowed out the earth under a bank with a tree on it and there was a root sticking right out. Itseng had just life enough in her to catch the root and hold on to it. She got her head out of the water, coughing and spluttering, and Tsheko reached over from the bank, with the bridegroom holding on to his legs, and managed to catch her by the arm. The river pulled and pulled as if it wanted her, as if it could not bear to let her go. A bit of the bank crumbled away under Tsheko's chest, but he did not let go. He hauled her up the bank and on to dry land. They held her so that she could cough and cough and spit out the muddy water. How wet she was— wet and cold!

"The kid?" asked Itseng through her coughing. One of the girls said it was drowned, swept away. But the kid had been lucky too. It had been swept toward a sandbank on the other side of the river and had managed to creep out. Now it was shaking itself and bleating. "Look, there it is!" said the bridegroom.

"Go over and get it! You said you were going to the

other side of the river—go now!" said Itseng. "If you do not get me the kid, you are not my husband any longer! I shall marry Tsheko. It was Tsheko who pulled me out."

"But I am your uncle!" said Tsheko. He had been one of the play uncles in the play marriage. Itseng stood up and shook herself just like the kid. The sun was beginning to dry her again. Children who had run away began coming back. The flood had not drowned her. "Very well," she said. "Then I will not be married at all!"

10

Out to the Lands

The floods went down. The mud dried. The river flowed slowly from pool to pool, retreating a little every day. Soon you could cross it again at the drift;* it came halfway up the legs of the oxen and nearly to the axles of the wagons. The houses were no longer on islands. But the bad cracks in the ground stayed and gaped. A few people filled some of them in with branches, but most were just left. The children learned to go around them or jump over them.

And now green leaves came, pushing through the mud,

* A ford in a river.

budding on the bushes. Flowers followed—many, many kinds, short and tall, big and tiny. Yellow or white flowers ran along branches; there were sweet smells everywhere. Marsh birds ran about the mud: water hens, teal and wagtails, and the tall, high-stepping herons. But when it was dry again, they moved on. The swallows, which had spent the summer in Northern Europe, perhaps nesting in the eaves of Scottish farmhouses, had swept south with the first cold days of October and now were back in Africa, where they darted and swooped in the sun again, round trees and rocks. There was singing at dawn now, not just the din of cocks crowing, but all the little pretty birds, waxbills and warblers moving in the branches, and the brown-crested bulbuls going through song after song. Above all, the grass came. The cattle ate and ate and grew strong for the plowing. Families prepared to move out to the land and plow. Maswe came over to tell Mother, who knew she must go, because Mualefe would plow his brother's land as well as his own, as they had agreed before Letsie went to the mine. So she must be there for the sowing and then to hoe the weeds. She would take baby, of course, and Modise, but the girls must stay with Granny and go on with school. They could walk out at the weekend; it was not much more than ten miles. She hoped Maswe would not order her about too much—Maswe with her man and she herself without hers. And still no letter.

The girls and Granny would look after one another. They were good girls. Granny could make the porridge. One fire would do, less wood for the girls to have to fetch. "If a letter comes—" she began to say to Mosaye.

But Mosaye said quickly: "We will get it to you at once —at once. I myself will do that."

So Mother got into the ox wagon with her small bundle and her hoes and baskets, the heavy baby on her back. Once the corn was sown, it would come up quickly, and so would the weeds. All must be ready. She had her blanket rolled under her and sat there while the whip was cracked and the oxen heaved themselves forward and the long, heavy wagon began to move. Modise was right in front shouting at the oxen, but they paid no attention to him.

The two girls sniveled a little that evening, but Ditla-beng was a cheerful place now, with everyone going off to plow and speaking of what they would sow and the good harvest they were sure to have. They greeted the chief with pleasure, half thinking that it was he who was leading them into plenty.

Mualefe had a fortnight's leave from the store; he was away at his land all that time plowing and mending the bush fences. The main crops of *mabele* and beans were sown, but Maswe and Mother each had a small field of their own, a woman's field with mixed maize and sweet-cane and melons growing through them. Segwai and the two schoolboys were left behind in Ditlabeng. Segwai had a boyfriend who was goalkeeper for the secondary-school team; she always went to the matches with the other girls and shrieked and jumped and waved her scarf with the rest of them, but when her boyfriend saved a goal she almost went mad. Now that her father and mother were both away, he came rather too often to the house. But Granny heard of this and went over and sat there. He was not the boy to treat her with disrespect, and indeed, if he had done so, Segwai would have been angry. But now he did not come so often or stay so long.

The bustle went on. The ox wagons of the families moved out to the land in a great shouting and cracking of whips and rattling of chains. There were six or eight pairs of oxen to each wagon, but the lead oxen mostly knew what to do. Tsheko's family moved out in their ox wagon, but Tsheko himself took his donkeys and their cart and went to and from when anything was needed. Once he picked Itseng up from her mother's little house on the land and brought her back with him to Ditlabeng, teasing her,

saying, "I'm your uncle, you must respect me." The donkeys
were getting plenty to eat now and went quite fast. Itseng
was usually the one who went off to the land to bring back
food that Mother had cooked. Out at the land there was

often meat, even if some of it might have come from a
tough old buck. There were roots too, which could be
boiled, and soon there was a growth of tender, wild spinach
leaves. Itseng would take home a big basket full of these

and Granny cooked them with salt. She said they were good for one and at least they were very good to eat.

Three weeks later there was more rain, not so much but enough. Oh, this would be a good season! But would it go on? Was this the beginning of good times? Still no letter.

"Will Father know at the mine that we have had rain?" asked Itseng. But who could tell?

Miss Mary sent for Mosaye. She had a letter in her hand and was very excited. The letter said that her Danish friend was coming; she would get off the train at Craigs and hire a car. "It would be better to find a lorry," said Mosaye. "The road is bad since the floods, too bad for a hired car. But when is she coming?"

"I am not sure," said Miss Mary. "Oh, letters take so long! Let me think. Perhaps—oh, it could be today! What shall I do?"

"Will she be angry?"

"I do not think so. Yet someone can be happy and goodhearted in a country like Israel, but coming here, who knows? Europeans can be difficult. We Africans can be blamed for anything. And if she does not find a hired car which will come out here—oh, I had wanted it to be so good for her! And I have at last got bricks for a kiln. I wanted her to see—!"

"Yes," said Mosaye. "Praise is a better sauce than meat.

Miss Mary, do not be so upset. Do not cry. Look, I am your pupil; it is not right that I see your tears. Listen, there is a car coming."

"Whose car is it?" said Miss Mary, and her fingers tapped jumpingly on the edge of the table.

Mosaye looked out. "It is Chief Letlotse's car. He will be going over to see his sister." She looked again. "But the car has come off the road—it is coming here—how it is bouncing! Oh, Miss Mary, Miss Mary, there is a white person in it!"

And there was the car drawing up, and out of it coming the chief, and then a woman—but wearing trousers like ladies in newspapers—with very yellow hair and a big hat and a bag with patterns on it, and she was laughing with the chief and he was taking out her parcels and her suitcase. "Oh, it is, it is!" said Miss Mary. "Bolette, you have come!" And she ran out and threw her arms around the yellow-haired woman.

The chief leaned against the wall of Miss Mary's little *lapa*. "God was on my side for once," he said in English.

"Or on mine," said yellow-hair. She was not looking severe and angry as most white women did, but instead she was smiling a great deal, especially at Chief Letlotse. "Do you know, Mary, I got to Craigs and the train had been so hot and I had no idea what to do and I had begun to ask how to get to Ditlabeng and all of a sudden appeared a charming young man—"

"And we bounced and bumped for three hours, so now we know one another well," said the chief.

"And we sat under a nice tree and drank beer and ate biscuits. But this export beer I do not like. One day he must try Carlsberg!"

"Some day," said the chief. "But you will bring her to see us, Miss Mary." Then he took the hand of the yellow-hair and said, "Goodbye, Bolette," and she said, "Goodbye, Letlotse." They seemed to take a long time smiling at one another and shaking hands. Miss Mary looked surprised. This was not the way for the chief and a white woman to speak with one another. Mosaye crept out of the house and then ran hard, back to her own place.

Miss Mary was anxious and uncertain. Had she done the right thing? She had made up a bed and emptied a drawer and put clean, white paper into it. She had taken away two of her own dresses so that there were hangers too, but would it do? Was it enough? But yellow-haired Bolette from Denmark seemed not to worry. She unpacked and talked and gave Miss Mary news about friends overseas. She had brought her a shirt and a woven square for a cushion and some very good sweets with silver and gold

106

paper round them. But the best thing she had, done up in a parcel, was the frame for a small loom, the kind for making scarves. "We will set it up," she said, "and then you will see how a big one must go. You must get someone to make it for you." But can I, thought Miss Mary, can I?

Who? Well, I will try. They talked and talked and Miss Mary made tea and in a while Bolette said, "And your potter?"

"Perhaps it is too hot to walk," said Miss Mary. She did not like to say that there was a thing which might make Mmaletsie not like her guest. Which indeed might not be liked by most of the old ladies of Ditlabeng.

"No, it is cooler now. Let us go," said Bolette. "I have been too long in the train. I am stiff. I would like to walk." She got up and stretched and then she said, "But first I will put on a cotton dress." So she took off her trousers and put on a cotton dress with a striped skirt. It was not a very long skirt, but still, thought Miss Mary, it will do, it will do!

11

Bolette Comes

Mosaye did not tell her grandmother at once; she had to
let it go slowly through her own mind. She did her homework and then she and Itseng pounded corn for tomorrow.
It was only then that she went over to her grandmother's
house and after greeting her began to explain that the
Danish lady had really come and that the chief had brought
her back from Craigs in his car. Mmaletsie snorted, "And
this car did not run into a tree! And nothing was broken!"
But Mosaye pretended not to notice. "This white lady, she
is how old?"

"I cannot tell at all. White people all look alike until one knows them. But I do not think she is very old, Ngoko."

"And she was wearing what? A hat?"

"Yes, yes, a broad hat like a very huge leaf."

"And her dress?"

Mosaye decided to say nothing about the trousers. "It was a kind of green with some yellow bits. Oh, it was modern! She had a chain on her neck which was, I think, silver, well made, and she had nice sandals. Also she had many small parcels. Perhaps she will open them."

Mmaletsie fidgeted. Suddenly she was not sure that she wanted to meet this stranger. She did not want to answer questions. Once the Mission ladies came and asked questions. How? Why? What? Not one of them had ever carried a pot on her head. They thought she was there to be pleased to see them and to answer their stupid questions. Old people should be respected and not questioned by younger ones. "Perhaps after all Miss Mary will not bring her."

"But why do you say that, Ngoko?"

"She will rattle and fidget. Whites are all the same. Tell the goat's granddaughter I do not wish to see this woman."

"Oh, Ngoko, you cannot say that! She has come all this way. She is an important person."

"When the big elephant crosses the river, it becomes small. I do not wish to see her."

"But I do!" said Mosaye, and suddenly she thought, I must fight, I must struggle. Granny does not want me to get away from Ditlabeng. She would like me to stay here as she has. She does not understand! "Ngoko," she said, "we cannot be impolite to a stranger who has come to our town. What would she think of us?" Mmaletsie hunched up and looked away. "Miss Mary is my teacher. She has taken trouble. She has written to this stranger. She has spoken much about the pots."

"These pots!" said Mmaletsie. "These worthless pots! They belong to the time that is dead. She will only want to ask me questions. I will break the pots. There will be nothing for her to see." And suddenly Mmaletsie seized one of the big pots and threw it against the wall of the *lapa*. It broke and scattered; there seemed to be bits of it everywhere. The noise of breaking stayed between them. She picked up another.

But Mosaye said, "That is mine, I made it. You shall not break it, Ngoko!" And she held on to the pot strongly with her two hands. Both of them breathed hard, the young

111

and the old, their faces close together. Then Mosaye heard voices coming near, one a strange voice. "She is coming, Ngoko," Mosaye whispered fiercely. And then, "She must not see us like this."

Granny dropped her hands from the pot. She was shaking all over. "No, my child, no." She sat down on the skin rug, staring out across the *lapa* from the step of her house. The sun was beginning to go down; it dazzled her eyes. There were tears but they did not fall.

Miss Mary and the Dane came into the *lapa* and walked over to Granny's house. The yellow-haired one no longer wore her hat, but she was wearing a skirt like a real woman; Mosaye was glad. Miss Mary nudged her and she gave the greetings rather shakily, but Mmaletsie acknowledged them, bending her head slightly.

"May we sit at your feet, Mma?" asked Miss Mary. Mosaye spread a skin rug; they settled themselves on it. The Dane began to stroke it, running her fingers along the pattern.

"Bring a chair, worthless one!" said Mmaletsie sharply. There was a chair in Letsie's house. It was his chair and Mosaye used it when she was doing her homework.

"They will bring you a chair, Bolette," said Miss Mary, pleased that they honored her guest.

112

But Bolette protested that she liked sitting on the rug. "It is beautiful. I wonder who thought of these fur patterns. Was it her?"

"She would rather sit on your beautiful rug," said Miss Mary to Mmaletsie, and then added quickly to Bolette that the rug had been made by the old lady's husband and that rugs were always made by men.

At last Mmaletsie was smiling a little. "That is good," she said. And then, "What is the name of your friend?"

"She is named Bolette," said Miss Mary.

"Bolette, Bolette," said Mmaletsie, feeling the name with her tongue. "That is a real name, a sensible name. It could be a Tswana name. Bolette. Yes."

Bolette was looking at the pots. She half put out her hand. After a moment Mmaletsie reached over to her with one of her small pots. Bolette turned it around between her fingers gravely, looking first at it and then across it at its maker. But why should she like it, thought Mmaletsie, she who can go to all the stores in the world with money in her purse? She cannot think any good of this home-made thing. And the same thought went through Mosaye's mind. Yet Mosaye also knew that sometimes the things in the stores were a nasty and ugly shape, but those that her grand-mother made were a good shape. And there were people

113

in the world to whom that mattered. She herself, she was beginning to look at things in this same way, so that she understood why this yellow-haired woman was thinking about her grandmother's pot with admiration. She reached over for the one they had been quarreling about. "That thing I made," she said in English. It was the first time she had used this school English to someone from overseas.

The Danish woman took it, felt it inside, put her fingers on to the fluting, then held it at arm's length. "It is a good one," she said to Mosaye slowly. "But there is much for you to learn still. If you would like to. Have you ever used a potter's wheel?"

Mosaye shook her head. "Miss Mary told me of this potter's wheel. I would like—to see."

"To see and to use," said Bolette. "And there is much else. The firing. The slip. The glazes."

"Slip? Glazes?"

"The colors you have seen," said Miss Mary, "on my small things."

"Yes," said Mosaye. "I would like to do that."

There was speaking after that between Bolette and Miss Mary and then between Miss Mary and Mmaletsie. It was explained that Bolette liked the pots very much, but she would like to know more about the making of them, especially the very big ones, the beer pots, which were so splendidly shaped. Would it be possible to see them being made, fired, and burnished? Mmaletsie said nothing for a little. Then she asked if the stranger would like first to see the mixing of the clays and powdered stone. Yes, she would indeed like that! Very well, tomorrow.

They took their leave and Bolette asked nervously if the

115

old lady would accept a little present. Again Mmaletsie did not answer at once. Then she held out her two strong, wrinkled hands cupped for the present. A whole packet of tea and another of sugar! Mosaye knew it was not good manners to seem surprised or pleased. The visitors left. Before tomorrow she and Itseng must get the clay and the stone and an extra pail of water. The borehole was running better now since the rain.

"Did she say she will stay here for many days?" asked Mmaletsie, smelling the tea.

"I think she will stay," Mosaye said.

"Then she will be able to learn," said Mmaletsie. "Child, go now, and put on the kettle. We will have tea."

12

The Letter

The next day something unheard of happened. Before school in the cool of the early morning, Miss Mary took Bolette to see the kiln she was building. There was a man there very slowly mixing mortar and laying bricks. While Miss Mary was at school, her Danish friend began laying bricks herself. The man stood back and stared at her. By and by, Chief Letlotse came on his horse. He got off and the man who had been laying bricks held the horse and saw this foreign woman showing the chief how to lay bricks, and the chief was laughing as though this was the most enjoyable thing in the world.

The story went round Ditlabeng. But Mosaye did not quite believe it. Still less did her grandmother, who had been slowly grinding down the stone to mix with the clay. But when Bolette came over and they all got down on their knees and began mixing, she started to think it might have happened. She herself was doing the translation between her grandmother and Bolette. It was exciting to have English suddenly coming real. Now that she was really meaning the words, she could remember them well. She said them better every time. They finished the mixing down on their knees, turning and thumping the clay.

"And the pit for baking the pots," said Bolette, getting to her feet, "where is that?" Mmaletsie said something half under her breath. "What was that, Mosaye?" Bolette asked.

Mosaye giggled. "She said that you should not make the sling to carry the baby until the baby is born. That is —what is the word?—that is a proverb."

"Well, then, tomorrow we make some pots. It is Saturday. You will be free all day. You will show me what you can do yourself. We shall all work together, we shall be like sisters."

Mosaye looked at her, nodded, and smiled. Oh, it would be lovely! She began to plan in her mind a dish she would make, with three short legs but not quite legs, more like foldings out of clay, which would balance and look well against the bulge of the side.

Perhaps Kabi would come back for two or three days. When he was so long away, Mosaye missed him. She forgot altogether how he had been tiresome and boastful and had run off to play instead of bringing in the wood. The last time Sello had been back, he had said it would be Kabi's turn next; he was turning into a good, sensible herd boy. When Molotsi shot a jackal, he had given Kabi the skin and shown him how to stretch it and cure it. One of the older men had promised to show him how to sew a skin rug, reminding him of the beautiful sewing that his grandfather had done. Yes, Kabi was doing well now!

The next morning Mosaye and Itseng got through the pounding of the corn and the sweeping of the house and the *lapa*. It was almost time for Bolette to come and the pots to begin coming alive out of the clay lump when the boy from the post office brought over a letter with a South African stamp. But was it from Father? It was not his writing on the envelope. Mosaye's heart jumped a beat. Who else could write? It must be something bad. It must be a letter saying he was hurt—dead—oh, she must take it quick, quick to Mother!

She turned it over and over. She did not dare to open it. She could not tell Granny. And oh, there were Miss Mary and Bolette coming over the road and it was her chance to show what she could do, her chance to escape, to be something different, to be their sister—and she could not take it. She would not be able to get her fingers into the clay, to the quick roll of the coil and the smoothing and shaping. She must go now.

As they came near and her grandmother moved into the door of her house to welcome them, all Mosaye's English left her. She could only show the letter with the South African stamp to Miss Mary and gasp that she would try to be back the next day—even perhaps that evening. But her mother might want her to stay. If it was bad news—and what else could it be? Then, without looking back, she ran.

What had happened, asked Bolette, and Miss Mary explained. "But the poor child! Going off with nothing to eat! Is it very far?"

"It is only fifteen miles," said Miss Mary. "But she should not run. That is stupid. She will only get too tired."

But she did run. She had put on the cotton dress in honor of Miss Mary and the Dane and the dress flapped at her legs, but if she wore it she was more likely to get a

120

lift, supposing there was anything on the road. After a while she slowed down a little. She was now a short way out of Ditlabeng on the way to the lands; the track had been made for ox wagons and the ruts had worn deep, made worse by the heavy rain but now filling up with sand again. It was hot walking, all the time not knowing what had happened to Father but knowing that she had missed her chance with the pots. The sun beat on her head; sweat patched the hard cotton. There was nobody on the road, though she could see people at work here and there in the fields. She went on walking. It would take her another four hours to get to the lands if she did not stop at all.

Then, behind her, someone shouted and she heard hoofs. It was Tsheko and the donkeys coming at a smart clip, the cart bouncing along the ruts. "Get in!" he said. "Your sister told me. We of the Bamatsieng must help one another." He reached down and gave her a hand in; as she sat back on the box top that made the seat, she began to know how sore her feet had been. "It is a bad letter?" he asked gently.

"I don't know," she said, "but I cannot see how it can be good." She stared out past the donkeys' ears. There was green on the bushes, and wide patches of growing grass here and there on ground which had been naked dust for

121

two years. The fallen fences of the land had green creepers growing through them. The crops were showing in all the fields that had been plowed early.

They took a fork to the right, then another to the left. "This white woman who has come to Ditlabeng," said Tsheko, "I think she has been to your house."

"She is there now," said Mosaye, and twisted her hands

together, trying not to cry. "She is with my grandmother making pots. She is a potter."

"That is strange," said Tsheko. "That is most strange. A white woman." And he shook his head. After that he asked Mosaye about school and what she was learning now. Did she do the multiplication tables? Could she teach him the tables for big numbers like seven?

Now they were at their own land. Tsheko tied the donkeys to a tree. Mosaye ran to the fire. There were Modise and Mualefe's two younger ones bringing in sticks, and a skinned buck hanging from a branch. "Where is Mother?" Mosaye shouted at them. Modise pointed to the end of the field. There were Mother and Maswe weeding among the young corn, bent over their hoes. Mosaye ran between the rows. Mother looked up and her hand went to her face, covering her mouth. Surely it must be bad news.

The letter! Mother opened it and the first thing that happened was that a note for one rand dropped out. Mosaye picked it up and began to read the letter across her mother's arm. Mother read slowly, speaking the words to herself. Mosaye read three times as fast, now and then looking up at her mother's face. The letter was written in pencil, badly. "A rock fell on my hand," wrote Letsie, "and I was off work. But I got my food. Only not my pay. It was tied up with many bandages by the doctor. I could not write, and when the bandages came off, the hand was very weak. But it is there still. It will be well. A friend will send this letter. I am lucky to have a friend. I shall work again soon. They say there has been rain. How is the plowing? Work well, my wife. I cannot send money yet. Greet the children, greet my mother. Stay well." At the end of the letter there were three sentences in another hand, the same that was on the outside of the envelope. "I am his friend. I am a Zulu. He speaks much about you and I have seen your picture so I send a thing for the children," and then a Zulu name which was difficult to read.

"So it is all right," said Mosaye. But she did not add— I need not have come. That was only in her mind.

"God has taken care of him," said Mother, "and sent him a friend."

13

Home

Mosaye came back with a load of wild spinach and a piece of meat from the buck. She had her mother's biggest basket to carry on her head, but it did not seem heavy. Her father was on his way back to health. The letter had not been bad in the way she had feared. And yet there was a pain in her mind. She found that Granny had kept a lump of clay wrapped in damp rags for her. Yes, enough to do for the dish which she had thought of! While Mosaye busied herself with it, and Itseng stripped the spinach leaves from the stalks and put them into the pot, Granny talked about her visitors. "Yes, she was a quick learner, was Miss Bolette! Quicker than the goat's granddaughter. She was not always asking, asking. She looked and felt and learned with her fingers. Yes, my child, I can believe now that she is truly a potter. But also I cannot believe that she is a white. Yes, yes, I have seen the color of her skin and her hair. That is not all. Magicians can change their shapes."

"But, Ngoko, she came from Europe, from far away. I saw the stamp on her letter."

"I have seen no white person with a heart like hers."

"I think there are others. The chief's sister, she says so. They write to her from London. Nurses from the hospital where she too was a nurse."

"My son will not speak so well of them when he comes back from the mines. Ah, my son, my son! Tell me again, child, what the letter said." So Mosaye told again about the letter and Granny shook her own hand about, whimpering a little, because of the pain in her son's hurt hand.

Bolette came on Sunday afternoon. She seemed to be as pleased as everyone else that it had not been too bad a letter and that Letsie was all right. And she liked Mosaye's dish, which was now drying off in the sun. Then, while they were sitting beside the pots, Bolette began gently questioning Mosaye about school and school fees and then about what she herself hoped for. After a while she said: "It is possible that there is another way out. Could you leave Ditlabeng and your family for perhaps a long time?"

"To go—to go overseas?" said Mosaye in a whisper.

"That is it. To learn to be a potter and also to go to school. Would you come?"

"With you?" asked Mosaye, and turned and looked at her, looked at her completely, the shape of her eyes and mouth, the strange bright hair. To go with her, to be so close, was it possible?

"That is what I was meaning," said Bolette. "But I must write to Denmark. It will take a little time, perhaps weeks. Meanwhile, you will go on working hard at school. And we will see how the pots turn out. Now, Mosaye, do you see the way that one of mine has sagged a little, it has gone to one side as if it was tired? That is because I am not used to working with coils. But it was most interesting to do. It was new to me."

"New things are interesting," said Mosaye. That was something she was sure about. But this other thing, she could not speak about it. She could not say to Bolette how much she wanted it. But she followed Bolette about as much as she could and imitated the way she spoke English.

"You must not say it like that!" said Bolette. "You will get a Danish accent!"

"I want to speak the same as you, the same as my Bolette mother," said Mosaye, "always."

Some of the pots came out of the firing well. Two of

Miss Mary's were cracked, and only one of Bolette's. Mosaye's came out beautifully. She put it into Bolette's hands. It was her gift, the best thing she had. Kabi came back from the cattle post for a few days, and even he was interested. He learned to say "good morning" and "good-bye" in English to Bolette. He had grown big and he boasted now of what he could do with oxen and how the bigger herd boys praised him. "If you go to school, you will become small again," said Mosaye.

"I do not choose to go to school," Kabi said. "School is no good to me."

"We will see what Father says," said Mosaye, and thought how sad Tsheko was because he was no longer at school. You did not miss school unless you knew what learning was and how it made you feel different. She would not like to have a brother who was only a herd boy. If it was a good year, then perhaps both Kabi and Sello could come back from the cattle post. Sello was over the age, yes, but surely the teachers, surely the government, must know there had been no money and would forgive him these few months?

Meanwhile, Kabi's hair had grown long and he had not combed it. Granny cut it and was disgusted at what she found in it; she made him wash it many times. It was shameful to be dirty. His father would be too ashamed to see him if he let his head get dirty. A Motswana must above all be clean.

The next week Chief Letlotse organized a hunt and took Bolette off with him in the lorry with the hunters and guns and dogs and a bag of meal and a drum of water and the other drum of gasoline and the spare wheel and the tin of salt and a bag of oranges and the tins of beer and the big box of cartridges. Bolette wore her trousers, but now everyone in Ditlabeng was used to her, and because they liked her they did not any longer mind what she wore. It was all right because it was she, and by now she could at least say the greetings properly. She had a camera and there were spare films inside her bedding roll. Letlotse had said he would teach her to shoot.

Out on the lands, the corn and beans were coming on well. Everyone would have a crop, although there were some lazy and stupid people who had not plowed yet in mid-December. But the weeds grew too, and in all the lands the women were busy with their hoes, starting in the early morning as soon as it was light enough to see, breaking off in the hot time, eating, and nursing their babies, then working again in the evening. Most families had brought in a cow at the same time as they brought in their plow oxen, so there was milk, and the farther out the lands were, the more likely one of the men was to shoot some game. It had to be hung high on a tree, out of reach of jackals or hyenas, and at night one must above all remember to bar the gate of the kraal wall so that no unwanted four-footed visitors could come in.

A few people had planted cotton. That was a crop which could be sold for much money, and the government adviser showed those who were willing to try it just what they must do and how they must spray and tend the cotton. Now it was coming up in rows, like little bushes. Some people, too, had been sent a few seeds from friends and were trying different things. One or two had a patch of sunflowers.

When Bolette came back from the hunt, she looked very happy and very brown; her arms were now browner than the inside of Mosaye's hands. That was nice. And she had taken many, many photographs, but they would have to go back to Denmark to be made into real pictures. And had the chief taught her to shoot? Well, she had put the rifle to her shoulder and he had held her hand over the trigger. But she was so sorry when the leaping impala buck had fallen down dead! Why? It was meat! Yes, but it was pretty and alive, said Bolette. She did not think she would like to be a hunter.

A letter had come for Bolette. How quickly her eyes ran through it! She read part of it to Mosaye. It was from a group of Danes who said they would educate this child and teach her to be a potter. It was too wonderful to be possible. Mosaye could not speak at all; she dropped her head into her hands and wondered if she would wake up. No, it was real.

On Friday after school she walked out to the lands to tell Mother. It was so different from last time. Even her feet did not tire.

Mother said nothing for a long time, though her Aunt Maswe exclaimed, saying how lucky she was. Suddenly she wondered if perhaps she had hurt Mother. Oh, why? "You will come back?" said Mother. "You will surely come back?"

"Yes, yes!" said Mosaye, and suddenly she was most sorry for her mother, for whom no gates had opened, as they seemed now to be opening for herself.

"You must go and say yes to the stranger!" said Maswe. "You must thank her. This is a thing we have not yet heard of in Ditlabeng."

So Mother came back with Mosaye, who took her at once to see Bolette at Miss Mary's house. At first it seemed that Mother could not speak to her. She could not look at her, even. Miss Mary tried to encourage her, but it was very difficult and Mosaye saw that Bolette did not quite understand. Mother took the letter in her hands while Miss

133

Mary explained it, trying to say where Denmark was, beyond Zambia, beyond Israel, beyond England.

At last Mother began to understand, to look at Bolette and to want to ask questions. "Where will the child live?" she asked, and Mosaye translated, hesitating a little because she felt that this was asking for something.

Bolette said: "With me and my sister. Look, here is a photograph of my sister. And Mosaye will teach me Setswana. I think now that I need to know it."

"Why?" asked Mother. "Are you coming back?"

"Perhaps," said Bolette, "perhaps." And she seemed to smile inside herself.

"We must ask my husband," said Mother. "I cannot answer. It is too big for me. It is almost nine months since he left. He will be here soon, soon."

"Well," said Bolette, "I am going to visit Lesotho, though I shall have to go through Johannesburg and I do not much wish to go there."

"Why?" asked Mother.

"Because we are all friends here," said Bolette, "but there they would stop us being friends. I will come back and get your answer."

14

To Go Is to Return

There was not another letter from Letsie, but people were saying that men who had gone at the same time as he were beginning to come back. Then one day, suddenly, just before New Year, there was Letsie getting down from a lorry which had come from Craigs. With him was another man. Those who knew what had been in the letter —and by now they were many—understood that this was his friend, the Zulu. They picked up their bundles and paid the driver. Letsie had still only his cardboard case, whatever was in it, but he had a second blanket. The

Zulu had a big tin box. How heavy it looked! But the Zulu did not seem to notice as he heaved it up. He also had a very big stick with a metal ring on it and a broad hat with a trimming of leopard skin. This was not ordinary leopard skin but the kind that is made in towns cleverly out of cloth. "Come," said Letsie, and set his face toward his own house. More and more people saw and told others; the older ones came to greet them lengthily while the boys and girls ran to tell Granny and the rest. School was almost over so the teacher let Mosaye and Itseng run home to greet their father.

One of the boys offered to go to the lands and tell them there. He did not get to the little kraal on the lands till dark, but Mother started before dawn with baby, who was a big child now, almost talking, on her back. Little Modise trotted beside her, sometimes getting a lift on her hip. Mother was back in Ditlabeng before midday. She got corn and brewed beer; friends brought meat. It was a very good time. Father was still weak in his right hand, though it was getting stronger, and now that he was home, it would surely become altogether strong. He had brought back little things for the girls and no more than a head scarf for his wife. There was no knife for Kabi, only a bag of sweets. But they all knew how it had been.

Still, his friend, the Zulu, had brought presents—a mirror
in a gilt frame that was certainly handsomer than anything
any of the neighbors had, pink and blue plastic combs,
necklaces of bright colors, and sugary biscuits. There was

also a small clockwork car for Modise; every child in the ward came to see it and touch it with one finger. When you draw your pay at the end of your term at the mines, there are dozens of people waiting to sell you all these things. White people, yes, asking you to buy. You could almost think you were doing them a favor, so sweet are their words! No, the Zulu was not going back to Zululand, not this time. His parents had died, his sister was married in Soweto. Who wanted to go there? Besides, they would perhaps not give him a pass. And then too, a man must travel and see the world.

Letsie and Mother had not let anyone see how glad they were to be together again. But when all the visitors were gone and the Zulu was asleep on his mat at the far side of the room, then they could speak with one another. "I meant to bring back much money," Letsie said. "I thought I would have the price of two good cows. But the rock slipped and my hand could not earn the money. I do not know what we can do about school fees. But it is in my mind that if Mosaye, my eldest born, does well in her primary leaving examination, she must stay on. Somehow."

Then Mother told him about the yellow-haired stranger from Denmark and what she had offered. Letsie said nothing for minutes, then he asked: "Does my child wish to go?"

"She wishes it very much," said Mother, and Letsie nodded.

It was a while yet before Bolette could be back from Lesotho. What was to happen about Kabi? After Father had been to the chief's house, bringing his friend, and greeted him and drunk beer with him, he went out to the lands and looked at the crops. Mother came with him, for the hoeing had to go on. Letsie wished they too had planted cotton, but Mualefe had not liked to risk it. Still, they were sure to get a crop and to be able to sell some of it; the first beans would fetch a good price. Then he went to the cattle post. The young heifer was in calf; that was something. Kabi said he did not want to go to school, but his father said: "All the same, you are going." But he was not yet sure. Could the school wait until the crop was sold so the school bills could be paid?

Meanwhile, the Zulu was his guest. Mother cooked for him and washed his shirts. He was a big man, very broad across the shoulders; he made funny mistakes at first when he spoke Setswana, but he was a splendid singer, and he knew so many Zulu songs that the *lapa* was crowded every

139

evening. The children learned to sing them too, with the click sounds that come into the Xhosa language. He had made a kind of flute out of a piece of metal pipe; it had made Sundays pass well when he played it, back there at the mines. But it needed drums and there are no drums in

Botswana. Still, most of the boys found tins that could be beaten, and another made an accompaniment with a string that thrummed on to an old tea chest. And then, sometimes, the Zulu told the young ones stories about the Zulu heroes, about Shaka and Dingaane and Cetewayo and those who came after them. New Year is a good time at Ditlabeng, and the Zulu was part of it.

And it seemed to happen that Segwai became less interested in football and much more interested in the Zulu. In a while there was talk of a wedding, not yet but when Segwai had passed her Junior Certificate, so that she would always be able to find some kind of job. And where would they go? "If I could come here to live, most certainly I would," said the Zulu, "for I like to be free. But there are more bad years than good and I do not wish to starve. If there were mines I would come, for I have good knowledge of mining. But there are no mines."

"It is said there will be mines," said Mualefe, "copper mines. The chief told us so. And also it was in the newspaper."

"If mines open in Botswana, I will come," said the Zulu, "and I will be a man of the Bamatsieng, for are we not all brothers?"

"You are truly my brother," said Letsie.

141

"And my younger son," said Granny, who had been listening.

And now Bolette came back from Lesotho and many people in Ditlabeng came over to Miss Mary's house to welcome her. When they were told that soon she would be going back to her own country, the women brought her presents, so that she would go back happily. They brought her woven baskets and pots, but none were as good as Granny's pots, of which now Bolette had many. Tsheko, who was clever at this, brought her spoons he had carved himself out of softwood. And Chief Letlotse gave her a very special and beautiful skin rug.

Letsie had been shy of Bolette at first, because of the white people he had seen in South Africa, who had not been of her kind. But at last he said yes, he would give her his daughter. Bolette took Mosaye into Craigs for a whole day, first to the District Commissioner's office to see about her passport; there were many questions, and photographs had to be put on to pieces of paper. Why? asked Mosaye. Bolette could not really explain. "One day," she said, "we shall be able to go where we like without all this nonsense. It is only a small world."

Then they had sausages and chips and soft drinks, and then they went to the big store. Here Bolette bought Mosaye

142

a dress and a warm coat and socks because it would be cold in Denmark in January. But they could wait until they got there to buy jerseys and thick stockings. It was most strange to go into shops with Bolette. She was not at all one to take the thing which the shopkeeper wanted her to take. Mosaye or Mother would have been frightened to ask for something warmer or of a different color or shape. But to have money means not to be frightened. That, thought Mosaye, is the best thing about money. The coat was made truly of woolen cloth, with a belt and great pockets. Mosaye looked at herself in a long mirror in the shop and laughed because this was someone she did not know.

"Shoes we must get," said Bolette, looking at the list she had made.

Mosaye said: "I have the canvas shoes I wear sometimes for church; they will do, please. They have no holes. It is cold here in winter, truly cold, but I have never worn shoes for school." Then she took a breath and said: "Instead of shoes, *Mma* Bolette, could we have the money for Kabi for one term? We do not know if the school will take him without money, even though we hope for a good crop."

Bolette put one arm around her and said: "You are my daughter now and you shall give Kabi a whole year's school, which I will pay for. But I am not having you come out

143

of the airplane at Copenhagen and having your toes nipped off by frost and snow, which are bad giants there, though very beautiful."

So it came about that Mosaye had shoes and these new clothes which were shown to all her friends. Itseng would be able to have Mosaye's gym tunic for school. In the end, Granny gave Mosaye the best of her skin rugs to wrap these beautiful things in, and it was tied with a strong cord. The pots were packed between grass into baskets, to go the long way by boat. But indeed Bolette had so many presents from her friends in Ditlabeng that it became truly difficult for her to know how she could take them back.

There is a proverb in Setswana: *Mayo ke maboyo:* going, I return. How often it is true! Chief Letlotse whispered it, lightly, to Bolette. Life is long; there is time for everything.

Mosaye and Mother, holding on to one another for a moment on the platform as the big train puffed slowly in, knew it was certain. And the people of Ditlabeng, they knew that one of their daughters had been fortunate and would come back one day and share the knowledge she had gained and the good things that came her way with her brothers and sisters, the men and women of Botswana.